DR. P-BODY

O'mia Tylet

DR. P-BODY

Copyright © 2025 by O'mia Tylet

All rights reserved. No part of this publication may be reproduced, stored in a retrieval system, or transmitted in any form or by any means—electronic, mechanical, photocopying, recording, or otherwise—without the prior written permission of the publisher, except for brief quotations used in reviews or scholarly works.

ISBN:
978-1-964061-32-0 paperback
978-1-964061-41-2 hardback

Library of Congress Control Number: 2025943313

This is a work of fiction. Names, characters, businesses, places, events, and incidents are either the products of the author's imagination or used in a fictitious manner. Any resemblance to actual persons, living or dead, or actual events is purely coincidental.

Cover design by: Nabin Karna
Interior design and layout by: Nabin Karna

S.H.E. PUBLISHING, LLC
Published by SHE Publishing LLC
Indianapolis, Indiana
www.shepublishingllc.com
info@shepublishingllc.com

Printed in the United States of America
First Edition: July 2025

This book is dedicated to all of us who suffer in silence,
struggling to forgive what we cannot forget.

In loving memory of my dear friend Andy Martin, whose passion
for storytelling and exceptional leadership inspired me daily.
You will never be forgotten.

Contents

To live is to suffer,
to survive is to find some
meaning in the suffering.

~Friedrich Nietzsche~

Chapter **1**

*H*ow did I get here? Where did I go wrong? As I sat in that 6x8 cell waiting on judgment, I started thinking about all I'd done. Then I heard the guard yell, "Hicks, you're up!" My walk to the courtroom felt like forever. As I entered the room, I looked back at my mom and everyone who came with her, then a flood of sadness came over me. *What a disappointment I must be to her,* I thought. After five minutes of lawyer talk, the judge asked, "Is there a plea in motion?" and both attorneys answered, "Yes."

I had spent years planning, strategizing, and crafting the perfect plan to right wrongs. I never viewed my actions as evil or psychotic—only as justified vengeance. Thinking of all the victims who had been violated, disrespected, and destroyed in one way or another left me without remorse. In fact, it brought joy to my heart to watch those men get exactly what they deserved.

"How did I get here?" I ask. Well, I guess I need to go back 18 years from today—back to when I thought my life was over and not worth living. Life was never kind to me. From the age of six, everything and anything began to show up in ways no child should ever have to endure. I grew up in a home with both of my parents, but the relationship with my father was unusual. He was military-strict, and my mother's OCD tendencies seemed attracted to his discipline. Everything had to be spotless, and in its place, or we would feel his wrath. I trusted my father and believed my mother knew what was best for us, so the extra attention he gave me—I welcomed.

We all had different bedtimes, but my nights were so uncomfortable. My father would always make a point to check that my sheets were off the floor and tucked, and each time it was. There were nights when he thought I'd forget to tuck so he'd creep into my room to find other things to look at. One night my dad pulled my panties aside and felt the moistness that came from my vagina. It felt strange but I thought maybe he wanted to make sure I bathed properly. This went on for a while until one day I spoke up and said "dad, no need to check me I'm clean". He snatched my undies and said, "shut up before I whip your ass". I grabbed my sheets and covered my head out of fear and didn't speak a word.

One night my mom caught him in my room masturbating with his penis in one hand and my panties in the other. She grabbed my lamp and threw it right to his head yelling "get the fuck out of my house". My mom threw all his clothes out our front window and threaten that if he ever came back, she'd shoot him with her 45. He left our home, and my mom cried for days. She blamed herself for his actions and later fell into a deep depression.

The madness didn't stop there; I later went to live with my grandmother who would periodically leave me home alone. One night she left to go to the store and told me to stay in her bedroom until she returned. I waited and waited and soon fell off to sleep. Granny had brought her male friend home, and he found his way to my room. That night he raped me and thanked me for my service. As I bled through my panties, I slowly walked over to my granny showing her my swollen, bloody vagina. She looked at me and said dry your eyes, he was doing what men do. She had sold me off in exchange for drugs she couldn't afford. After several months of this, my mom got herself together and saved me from that nightmare. I never said a word of this to her as I didn't want to risk losing my mother again.

At this point, my self-esteem was so low I'd always say to myself, *what could a Black girl like me possibly contribute to this world?* I'm poor, nothing special to look at, insecure, easily manipulated, and I'd probably end up following the same path as every other girl in my neighborhood. I guess my thoughts weren't too far off—there weren't any successful women on my block that I could look up to or talk to. I spent most of my time watching television, living vicariously through the characters and their lifestyles. I inserted myself into *The Cosby's* as a child; as a teen, it was *Three's Company*; and as an adult, I was drawn to medical shows I could imagine myself in. I was so lost in my imaginary world that I wrote out what life might look like for me—if I ever made it out of the ghetto.

Who am I? I'm Dr. Jaylee Hicks; college graduate, magna cum laude, and the only one in my family to start a successful business. The youngest black female doctor in Bridgetown County to have over 100 employees with multiple locations. I must say, I did well for myself despite my past. Unbelievable huh? Well let me tell you a story about a woman who went from a successful doctor to a Felon.

"Beep, Beep!" "Come on Chick, let's go!" I yelled. It had been months since I partied with the girls, as long study nights, finals and researching locations for my soon to be Dr. P-Body Clinic kept me pretty busy. Racquel ran from her 2-story porch and made her way to the car. *"Congratulations bitch or shall I say Dr. P-Body.* Racquel always exaggerated her entrance. *"Yea, I'm bragging, my best friend is a successful Doctor,"* she said. "Thanks girly, I've worked my butt off, and it's finally paid off, but tonight, it's party time!" I said with excitement.

Racquel and I chatted the entire ride. Reminiscing on the good old days, discussing current events and planning future moves. Our bond was unbreakable. She and I met through a mutual friend at the age of 12 and were college roommates at BU. At the beginning, college felt nice, Raquel and I bonded instantly, I was finally away from a horrible upbringing that would have led me to alcoholism, drug abuse, even a sexual drive that would be so high prostitution looked promising. I was finally happy until…………...

My second semester at Bridgetown University became a reminder of something so dark, I stopped recognizing myself after a while. One night, Raquel and I were studying late at the library with our heads buried in books, and that's where I met Michael L. Raquel noticed us staring at each other and said, "Girl, go talk to him." So I did—and what can I say? I fell for his eyes. He wowed me, and it felt right. His qualities were different from all the others, but the one that sealed it was his *consistency.* He showed me around campus, introduced me as his lady, and was well-liked by many professors. I had no reason not to trust him—until we received an invite to a mutual friend's jazz session (*a different scene for me, since I was only familiar with wild house parties*). We drank wine and chatted for hours; it was the perfect date. What started out perfectly ended in horror. I was found on the rooftop of the jazz bar, bottomless, with a sign that read "You asked for it." Raquel never got over it and blamed herself for what happened to me. Maybe that's why she still has trust issues today.

As we were approaching Elana's party, Raquel said, *"Damn girl, Elana's party is lit"*, while hanging her head out the window of my car. Elana had turned 30 and wanted to celebrate in style. Her music was loud, the yard was packed and nothing, but smoke was coming from the grill. '*Shot, shots, shots!*' Elana yelled as we walked towards her. Racquel grabbed her shot without hesitation, but I knew I'd have to either limit my drinks or schedule a Share ride home and send for my car the next day.

"Bitch, you're acting funny because you're a doctor now. Grab the Cîroc shot and let's drink!" Elana said while pushing the shot plate towards my chest. Elana always made sure her parties had everything her attendees wanted. After 2 shots, I decided I'd

reach my max, so I sat by the DJ booth and sipped water. I felt a weird stare coming from across the room, so I walked over to this dark piece of deliciousness and just like that we were in deep conversation.

"Hello, I'm Jaylee and right as he was about to speak, I interrupted him and said, *"Don't tell me, you know me from somewhere huh?"* He chuckled and said, "Hi *I'm Keith and no, I do not know you from anywhere, but I'd like to get to know you.* We exchanged numbers and started dating a couple of months later. Life felt right with him. But after a while he couldn't grab hold of his ego and became aggressive. His charming demeanor went from sweet to controlling and verbally abusive. Usually, those red flags would appear to me early on, but it took a while for me to notice them, or it went unnoticed because I didn't want it to end.

After 2 years of his roller coaster personality, I decided enough was enough; I was ready to leave the relationship for good. I found out later that he had taken huge amounts of money from our account paying rent for his other family for an entire year saying he was investing to triple our income. His dishonesty left me damn near bankrupt, so I packed a few outfits and stayed nights at different hotels. He would call and leave lots of messages until I threaten to file an Order of protection if he didn't leave me alone. Closer to the end, I had started spending lots of time at my clinic. Dr. P-Body Clinic was my safe place and had become my entire life.

I had not heard from Keith in months at this point, so I was able to build my credit and my account to purchase a 2-bedroom condo on the east side with big bay windows on the 22nd floor that looked over the city and it felt good. After 4 weeks of being in my home and doing things my way, I started feeling a bit better about my decision to leave the relationship and got back to doing what I loved "Research". I started looking into curing Erectile Dysfunction because of my late uncle. His wife had left him for another man because of his inability to perform so he killed himself. I was determined to find a cure so I made space in my lab filled with information and samples to create a serum that would cure men biggest fears. After two years of testing the results looked promising so I started finding ways to patent my creation and later it became LH Vitamins.

On my way to the clinic, I noticed an unusual amount of traffic. Mondays are usually smooth on the freeway, but this Monday traffic was bumper to bumper. Where is everyone going this morning? I asked myself as I headed to the clinic. Then I heard the radio cast say, *"An accident on rte3 has caused a pile up"* so I blasted my music and fought through that hour-long drive. "Good morning, Katherine," I said after arriving at the clinic, looking frustrated after that drive. *"Hello Dr. Hicks, looking at your face, you must have got caught in that traffic,"* she said. "Girl yes," shaking my head. "What does our day look like?" I said. *"Busy as usual"* she replied.

Katherine was the head receptionist at the clinic. She and I met during my last semester at BU. She was a volunteer at the trauma center for women (where Raquel had received therapy). Raquel introduced us after her 6-week completion ceremony, and we clicked instantly. She had majored in business then went to work for a prestigious accounting firm after graduation. The company bamboozled her by stealing her ideas then letting her go. They used the excuse they were phasing out her department to fire her. With her sorority connections, she filed a multimillion-dollar lawsuit and won. Katherine always talked business, but she was way more than talk, so it was no surprise when she heard about the opening of my clinic that she became a silent partner.

She always wanted to stay involved in the day-to-day, manage the staff, my schedule and daily load. She never wanted others to feel intimidated by her, so she decided to become head receptionist /executive assistant. Katherine has a charm like no other. She would make patients comfortable, and they loved her.

Our first patient arrived, and it was Mr. Ramon. A regular I'd diagnosed with Erectile Dysfunction months ago who'd come in for a regular visit and prescription refills. He would also request a month's supply of our LH serum that would allow him to stay erect for 4 hours. This temporary fix helped his marital issues but made it problematic at the same time. *"Good morning, Ms. K, I'm here on time as usual,"* he said with a smile. *"Good morning Mr. Ramon, have a seat and the doctor will be with you soon,"* Katherine gathered his file so that he'd be next to call.

10-minutes into waiting Mr. Ramon asked *"Ok, Ms. K, how much longer?"* he said as he nervously shook his leg. *"You're up soon, here's the remote, feel free to watch what you like until they call your name."* We provided informative pamphlets for our patients and our televisions were set on 24-7 sports shows with intermediate commercials showing our many services and how we could help.

"Mr. Ramon you're up," said nurse Daisy. Daisy was our head nurse, who took her job seriously and who was determined to prove herself. She and I met at a nurses and doctors convention. We partnered up in the clinic mock trial and came in first place. I was pleased and wanted to get to know her more. We'd talk and she'd mention how she always wanted to be a nurse. She explained how she worked as a waitress to finish nursing school. It wasn't enough, so she stripped at night to make ends meet. I can tell she was ashamed, but I was the last to judge, so I embraced her while we continued our talk. We learned we had a lot in common; for instance, we were from the same town. She'd intern at a local hospital that she didn't really care for, but she'd mentioned how the doctors were mean and didn't care about teaching. She seemed sincere, she showed great character and had a lot of passion, so I offered her a job.

Daisy had prepped his room and left a new disclosure form in his view to complete. *"Mr. Ramon, please complete and sign these forms and the doctor will be with you shortly."* Daisy handed him a pen and left the room. After 15 minutes of patiently waiting, I knocked softly on the door. "Mr. Ramon, how are you?" I said as I went inside. *"I'm ok,"* he replied. *"Just a bit concerned about "you know what",* pointing to his penis. It seems my symptoms are getting worse, and your LH serum isn't working.

"No worries, lets chat a bit more about what you're feeling, maybe run a few tests then take it from there." I've heard many stories such as his, so my course of action plan was already in mind. His concerns were mental for the most part and with guys, all they need is a little reassurance that usually seals the deal for them. I spent another 10 min listening to him describe what he was feeling, ran a few tests, wrapped up his visit, then scheduled a follow-up appointment for two weeks out.

Watching him leave the clinic, I noticed he held his head low, mirroring his confidence. How sad must it be to have lost hope… nurse Daisy called my next patient, but something about Mr. Ramon's condition stayed with me. The samples in my lab came to mind and I said to myself I think I found my 1st study. My day was filled without breaks, so by 5pm, I was starving. Family and friends would always tell me, *"You must pour more into yourself in order to pour into others"*. I understood the message, just never applied it in my life.

Because of my fascination with Mr. Ramon's case, I wrapped up my last patient file and informed Katherine that I'd lock up when I leave that it would be a long night for me. She looked over at me and said, *"How come you always say the same thing to me and expect different results?"* We chuckled, because we both knew that the clinic was her baby as well and there was always admin paperwork that needed to be done or to prepare for. I walked towards the lab with several plans in mind and Katherine headed to her office.

While looking through my telescope, my phone beeped constantly. I remember Racquel had invited me to her backyard BBQ, so it was no surprise receiving 15 text messages demanding my presence. However, this new case attracted all of my attention at this point. As I contemplated calling Racquel back, I remembered a paper I wrote back in college, only this time I wanted to permanently stop ED, so I ran to our storage room, pulled down my "Item" box and took all that I had researched back to the lab with me.

Wait, let me text Racquel back before I get too caught up in this project I said to myself. As I was preparing the text, our business line rang (*we installed that line for employees only to report in and I forgot I gave my girls all my numbers in case of an emergency*). Thinking it was an employee calling off, I answered, "Dr. P-Body clinic." A frustrated voice yelled *"Skank I know you got my messages!"* It was Racquel being her crazy self as usual. "Girl, I've been so busy, I was about to hit send right as you called letting you know I wouldn't be able to make it", I said hoping she would understand.

Racquel was so distracted by the news she was about to tell me that she didn't respond to my declining of her invitation. She started rambling, but all I could think about was getting back to my research. She finally got my attention when she said, *"Girl did you hear what happen to Elana?"* My eyes popped open wide because Elana was a part of our 3 amigos crew. *"No, what happened? Tell me,"* I said. Elana is in the hospital. "What?" I said astonished. I couldn't imagine why she'd be in the hospital without anyone reaching out, so my mind started racing with anxiety.

It's been a while since we were all together. Being so busy with the clinic, I did not plan any time with the girls. "Racquel, y'all have my number, how come you didn't call like you're calling now?" She interrupted me and said, *"Girl, wait let me explain."* As she was explaining the start of this disaster, I couldn't believe what I was hearing. Elana met this guy, a truck driver while at the grocery store. They started dating and it went on for a while then things got serious. Elana gave him keys to her home so that while he was in town, they'd be together (he was an over-the-road driver for Trucking Inc.).

As she carried on, I started to think, damn, are there any good men today? "*Are you listening,*" she asked. Racquel knew me oh so well… if I stayed quiet for 61 seconds, I was drifting. "Yes, keep going," I said. Racquel would take so long getting to her point and just like any other story, she took forever to get to the reason for Elana's hospital visit. "*Girl, Ralpfy (Elana's boyfriend) was married and had been cheating with other women and later found out, men too. Ralpfy had given Elana a STD that compromised her reproductive system.*"

At the age of 32 with only 1 daughter, she was having a hysterectomy and would no longer be able to have children. The doctor informed her that the STD was dormant in her body without signs, Elana said. The disease had caused an infection so badly that the surgery was her only option. "Girl I'm so sad for her, I bet she cursed his ass out and even laid hands on him" I said knowing how Elana would fight in a heartbeat.

Racquel agreed and said, "I'm so hurt. Elana is usually careful and discerning, I'm shocked signs didn't come to her early." Elana's hope to have more children was ruined because of this lying man who would soon get his karma. I was tired of men using and abusing women for their pleasures and leaving them empty. I thought something had to be done about this. I could tell by Racquel's tone that Elana's condition hit her in a personal way, so as she was ending the call, she asked that we pray for her and schedule a time to visit Racquel after her surgery.

Beep, beep, it was my other line. I ended the call with Racquel to answer Katherine. *"Hello,"* I said. *"What took you so long to answer Jay"* Katherine said. "My bad, I was on an important call, what's up?" "I'm here at our favorite Chinese place would you like anything? You haven't had dinner, being stuck in the lab." "Yes, four eggrolls please." I was so distracted by the call I forgot to ask for a large Egg Foo Yung, I thought. Trying to get Elana's news off my mind, I went and grabbed 4 more specimens to research only this time my reasoning was different. Instead of only a cure creation I wanted a payback creation,

Hours had passed and Katherine had fallen asleep on her office couch. I thought *she was always trying to hang with the big dog.* I loved her loyalty and thoughts of not letting anyone leave the office late alone. I grabbed my sample case and the four valves to revise hoping for a value match but with no success, so I thought maybe I should go home and try again another time. I gathered my papers and grabbed 2 more samples to take home with me. I had a built-in lab in one of the bedrooms in my condo, perfect for spur-of-the-moment research. "It's 12:30am Katherine, let's head home," I said. Katherine gathered her things as did I and we locked up to leave. Katherine opened her 2024 Tesla Cybertruck and said, *"See you tomorrow, Jaylee,"* then I waved as we said our goodbyes.

As I pulled into my home garage, I looked at the time and thought *Damn, I have to get up in 5 hours,* so I disarmed my alarm and walked inside of my chilly home. I put both valves inside the rotation kit and decided to increase the temperature (which later produced 6 samples of serum and later became LH 2.0), turned the thermostat to 75 degrees and took a 5-minute shower. I went to bed praying for a successful surgery for Elana and a speedy recovery.

'Wakeup, Wakeup, Wakeup,' sounded my alarm. *Damn, is it 6am already*? I thought. As I yawned and stretched, I remembered last night's conversation with Racquel and decided I needed to get to work and help make a difference. I was curious so I went into my lab and to my surprise I had a value match. Excited to get to work, I ran 30 min on my treadmill, showered, dressed and then the fresh smell of Folgers came from my Keurig coffee machine, straight to my nose. I filled my cup, grabbed my purse and headed to the office.

"Good morning, Dr. Hicks, you're here early," Betty said. "Yea, I woke up ready to work," I said with a smile. "Where is Katherine?" I asked. *"She is in the washroom. Jessie is covering the front desk until she returns."* As I looked out into the waiting room, it was filled with patients, so I knew it was going to be another busy day. To no complaint, this kept me in business, but it saddens me how many men wait until the last minute to get a checkup.

"Good morning, Dr. Hicks" Katherine said. *"Did you get any sleep last night?"* "Yes, I did, I could've used more, but today I have this crazy boost of energy so hopefully it last. I noticed most of today's appointments are prescription refills and my usual 10 min questionnaire meet, this is great, it gives me more time to research. Katherine chuckled and shook her head. As I was preparing for my first patient, Jessie from administration informed me that Roselina from the wellness center had called four times in hopes that I had a few openings today for 4 of her intakes.

Jessie knew to confirm scheduling with me, but she also knew that we'd never turn the help center down. I had been a supporter of Roselina help center for years. She created a safe place for individuals who were struggling financially and in need of health care & nutrition. Roselina would provide patient documents 24 hours before so that I could be prepared, but this day was different. She had so many walk-ins she couldn't keep up. Helping Rosalina at the center was a huge contribution to the community now that health care is so expensive. I've always believed in giving back by helping, but the stories I hear started to affect me in unexplainable ways.

I decided to call her back while my next room was being prepared. "Hello, this is Jaylee, can I speak to *Roselina?*" I asked. *"Hey Hicks (she always called me by my last name) I'm sending over 4 intakes, is that ok for today?* She asked. "That's totally fine, just send over their Intake forms and Katherine will create their patient file with us here" I replied. *"Thanks Jaylee, I'll talk to you later,"* she said as we were ending the call.

Where there is anger, there is always pain underneath.

~*Eckhart Tolle*~

Chapter **2**

I could hear Daisy call for Mr. Jamerson to follow her to room 3, so I grabbed his file for a quick review. My mind was filled with anxiety as I read further; he was the perfect candidate for the payback trial. As I walked to the room, I knew that the woman who came in the office everyday ready to help others had started to fade away. At first, I only wanted to help men with their ED symptoms so that homes weren't wrecked from things they couldn't control, but with what happened to Elana and my past experience, my passion to hurt men became obsessive. What was once a temporary issue had soon become permanent.

I wanted men to think twice before giving themselves to women and then hurting them, so I created a serum that would send a shooting pain to the penis with every erection. Mr. Jamerson's file details made him the perfect candidate to receive a dose of my planned creation. His file read "ED, possible STD, currently active with 15 women, and married with children."

"Knock, knock, Hi I'm Dr. Hicks, how is it going?*"* "Hi, Dr. Hicks, I'm in need of some meds, something feels weird," he said shaking his head. "Well, I reviewed your file, and I have a few questions. For now, I'll get the nurse to run a blood panel and maybe get you a dose of antibiotics to help with the burning. I'll be right back... Daisy, can you please run a blood panel on Mr. Jamerson and let me know when you're done," I said while exiting the room.

Daisy grabbed her supplies and headed inside. *"Ok, Mr. Jamerson, which arm would you like me to use*?" He smiled and stretched his right arm out. Daisy had taken all she needed then waved to me that she was done. I had 6 samples that I brought from home and was anxious to use them. I grabbed a valve from my pocket, a LH Vitamin for blood flow along with an oral antibiotic and walked back to his room.

"Mr. Jamerson, I'm going give you a dose of antibiotic and our LH vitamin. It's a vitamin to help with blood flow to the penis, failing to mention I added a dose of revenge to his regimen. Your file reads 15 women you're sexually active with, correct?" He looked at me and said, *"I Know, I know, I just get caught up with the ladies then it turns into sex."* I turn to him and say, "Because of your symptoms, I'm concerned that it could've spread to your wife and that maybe she needs to see a doctor as well."

"No," he said firmly. *"My wife does not need to know, we haven't had sex in months so there's no need to alarm her."* "Mr. Jamerson, some symptoms could lay dormant in the body, I really think you should tell her."

He shook his head no, so I wrapped up his visit. *"Ok, we have your panel, we will send it to our lab and call you as soon as your results come in."* As I was leaving his room, I noticed that the waiting area started to pack. Roselina's referral intakes had walked in, and I couldn't be happier. I walked back to my office to record Mr. Jamerson's symptoms and to start a mini report on the administering of the new version of LH 2.0. Still unsure of its success but wanted to record, nevertheless. I grabbed the remaining 5 valves and put them in my pocket for the next eligible patients; unfortunately, the remaining patient profiles were not a good fit for the experiment. I was vengeful, but not hateful. My wrath was only to the men who I thought deserved it. 6:30pm came quickly and I had finished with my last patient, so I updated a few files and headed home.

The next two days were filled with our regulars and Rosalina's intakes. Katherine and I were both happy that we were one day closer to the weekend. Katherine had more joy than I, because her #1 rule was, she'd work Mon-Fri, Saturday was volunteer day at different centers and Sundays was her holy day. For me, my schedule looked very different.

I worked Mon-Saturday and Sunday was my Holy day and maybe I would see my friends. On Saturdays, Daisy and I would open the clinic from 8-12pm. Saturdays started out as catch-up days, paperwork, audit preparation (all that Katherine didn't finish) but then after a few Saturdays of being open I noticed the high call volume that came in requesting to be seen so we started seeing patients. I enjoyed Saturdays because we controlled our visits, so nothing was ever too crazy.

Elana was heavy on my mind, so I called Racquel and asked her to ride with me to see her before visiting hours had ended. *"Girl, yes, come scoop me up,"* she said. As I left the office I thought, *damn, I haven't eaten all day* so before grabbing Racquel, I stopped and grabbed Thai from our favorite restaurant Royal's. Pineapple fried rice and crab Rangoon was Elana's favorite. I knew after all that hospital food; she'd enjoy a good meal with friends.

As we pulled up to Lainey General Hospital, we decided to valet the car because the garage so too far to walk. *"Hello, were here to see Elana Weatherspoon, she is in room 404B,"* the receptionist looked frustrated as she created our labels. *"This machine has been acting up all day, please forgive my frustration,"* she said. *"Oh no worries,"* Racquel replied. As she pointed down the hall, she instructed us to follow the red arrow to the end of the hall and make a left, take the elevator to the 4th floor and the lady at the nurse's station will guide us to her room.

Racquel and I chatted softly about the ways of men and as we approached Elana's room, we saw she had been crying. "There is no crying in the hospital" I said jokingly. *"Oh, my goodness, I'm so happy to see you both. Being here all alone is so depressing. All*

I think about is the dumb mistakes I made", she said as she held her head down. We hung our coats and assured her everything would be ok. Racquel wiped down her table, spread the food out and we had a feast. We could tell by the way Elana sat up in bed that our presence was what she needed to smile again. We chatted, laughed, cried and laughed again and to us, that was the best feeling in the world.

Around 9pm, the nurse came in saying "Visiting hours are over." Sadness came over Elana's face, so Racquel shouted *"Girl, we will be back Saturday. Jaylee is off at 12pm and I don't work that day, so we'll have an entire day together, you just rest."* As we said our goodbyes, we kissed her on the forehead and left the room. *"I love you both,"* she said as we were walking away. We looked back, smiled and said, *"We love you more."*

I left the girls with a bit of rage. My need for payback became more intense because of the flashbacks that popped into my head from my past. Our friendship was more than a basic friendship; we were sisters, so when one hurts, all hurt. There were promises we made to one another as kids that we would always protect each other. A piece of me felt both Racquel and I didn't keep our end of that promise because of our busy lifestyles. The entire ride home, all I could think about was whether Mr. Jamerson showed any symptoms and what they were after his visit with me.

I dropped Racquel off at home and did 80mph on the freeway. The second I got inside; I grabbed my lab coat and went to work. I placed the first sample on the scope to see if anything had changed; everything looked the same as yesterday, so I walked to the kitchen for a cup of coffee (thinking it's going to be a long one). *"Pop, Pop"* a sound came from the glass under the scope. I was concerned, as I had never heard the popping sound before. The value match was the same, so I assumed the high temperature caused the popping sound. I gathered 10 more samples, labeled them LH 2.0, filled them with serum and went to bed.

"Wake up, wake up, it's work time," that damn alarm went off right as I was in a deep sleep. I was drained from the night before, so I took my time getting dressed. As a routine, I showered, grabbed my Folgers and avocado toast and headed to work. Traffic was a bit tight this morning, but wasn't surprising, as Fridays are always busy on the freeway. I figured this was a good time to gather my thoughts and think of new ways to speed up the creation of my serum (LH 2.0).

Then I thought, *let me call Katherine.* "Dr. P-Body Clinic, *how can I help you?"* she answered. "Hey Kat, I'll be there in 15min, how's our load?" I said, waiting for the light to change. "It's going to be a full house today, Roselina is sending 12 more intakes and some have already arrived." "Ok, I'll be there in a bit, " I said as I was ending the call.

It's happening, it's finally happening. I got another *value match this morning, I have samples I can use today, and I get to see Mr. Jamerson's results if they're back,* I said to myself.

"Good morning, Daisy, let me get situated and let's start with room 3 today. *"Ok, Dr. Hicks, long night huh?"* She asked with a chuckle. "Girl you already know." I was always laid back and cool with the staff. I wanted them to always to feel comfortable and confident because that made good workers who provided good service. *"Mr. Levi you're up, follow me to room 3,"* Daisy said as she grabbed some last-minute forms and informed him that I would be in shortly.

I decided to let Mr. Levi sit a bit so that I could review Mr. Ramon's results. I was anxious and nervous because I secretly wanted to label him as a good candidate for my curing trial but Chlamydia and trichomoniasis was the diagnosis that came up with bold red letters on his report. "Katherine, please call Mr. Ramon and schedule him an appointment for tomorrow," I instructed Kat while grabbing Mr. Levi's file. Mr. Levi needed a refill and my 10 min evaluation, so his visit would be quick, I thought.

I zoomed through each scheduled patient and then it finally happened. Looking through each file, I was able to pull 5 patients from the bunch to administer LH 2.0. Their intake papers show history of being constantly treated for STDs, so the carelessness of their health fit my criteria for the trial. I gave each of them 1 valve of LH 2.0 and the necessary medication to help their irritants.

Our phones rang constantly, from patients wanting to schedule Saturday appointments but due to our heavy load sent from Roselina's help center, we let some calls go to our answering service. Now that may have sounded cruel, but we offer online care access when our departments are unavailable, as well as 24hr chat access and an easy scheduling site.

The phones wouldn't stop; we tried ignoring the distraction, but it was overwhelming. *"Dr. P-Body, how can I help you?"* Betty said. *"Hi, this is Thomas, and I need to talk to the doctor right away, is Dr. Hicks in?"* he said in a panic. *"Can I ask what's this concerning*?" she asked. "*No! I need to come in, let her know I'm coming now,*" then he ended the call.

Betty then paged me to the conference room, warning me of Thomas's visit sometime that day. She looked worried, but I assured her that everything was ok and that she could go to her next patient. I updated the remaining files and sent their scripts to the pharmacy. From Betty's concern, I knew Thomas would be someone she'd want to avoid so I told Katherine to put him in room 5 when he arrives. My mind was racing, I had mixed feelings about his diagnosis, but selfishly I had other ideas in mind, like making him apart of my LH 2.0 trial.

About 20 minutes into my thoughts, I heard Katherine say, "*Thomas, please follow me to room 5*". He was given a hospital gown and forms to complete to describe his pain. He was also asked to undress waist down before I came in. I grabbed a valve and my notepad and headed in. "Mr. Thomas, from the message I was given, I could tell you were upset, what's going on?" I asked. "*Dr. Hicks, I'm experiencing something I never experienced before,*" he replied. "*Like what*?" I asked. He started to explain that it started with an Erectile Dysfunction issue that took him longer than usual to become erect. Then he said his erection lasted about 10 min, followed by a burning sensation every time he'd urine.

"I'm sorry for what you're experiencing, how often is this happening?" I asked. "*I noticed the burning when urinating about 2 days ago, but my erection issue seems to be getting worse.,*" he said, while holding his head down. "Well from looking at your pain sheet, I can tell you, your level 9 pain score could come from an STD, have you been having unprotected sex? Yes, he replied but only once. I did a quick view of his penis and let him know that I'd be prescribing him antibiotics with cream to help with the burning and run tests for other STDs. I also included a dose of the revised LH Vitamin for blood flow and possibly ED correction.

"I gave him 5mil of antibiotics and said he'll need to follow the directions on the label for the next 10 days even if he starts to feel ok. *"Dr. Hicks, what STD do I have?* He asked concerning. I replied, "Your symptoms *mimic Chlamydia with a UTI but the labs will tell for sure."* He didn't look as if he had heard of this before, but who knows, maybe he did and ignored it. *"Is this curable?"* he asked. "Yes, just take all your meds and always use protection please," I said, before leaving the room while he dressed.

Thomas's visit pushed us 20 minutes behind, but we made it work. There were a few more patients to be seen; thankfully they were all prescription refills. Katherine always knew how to schedule my appointments in case time got away from us or an emergency arose, so the delay wasn't bad at all. *"Ok, Dr. Hicks we are all done, I'm heading out,"* Daisy said as she wrapped up. "Hey, will you be in tomorrow?" I asked. *"Absolutely, I scheduled buffers for the floors, so I'll will be here to oversee them,"* she said. "Ok, see you tomorrow," I replied.

Katherine was also packing up to head home; she grabbed a few files to work on and so did I. *"You're leaving too?* I said. "Katherine nodded and said, "yes, what about you?"" "Yes, I have to be in here early tomorrow so I'm going home to rest." I grabbed my things, and she locked up behind me. I couldn't decide on what I wanted for dinner, but I remembered Betty telling me about the steak place down the street. I called and pre-ordered a ribeye and potatoes with a side of broccoli. I couldn't wait to get home.

The next morning, the sun shined brightly through my blinds then I heard the doorbell ring. "Who is it?" I asked. "Mr. Bailey, your doorman. I have a package for you." Really? This early in the morning? I thought. I opened the door, grabbed my package, thanked him for his service, closed the door, and got dressed for work. I rushed out, heading to the office, because I remembered—the buffers were coming, and there was a spot I wanted them to pay special attention to.

"Good morning, Daisy," I said as I glided through the office. "Girl, let me tell you…" she said in a gossiping tone. "Roselina has five intakes coming to the office today. I read their profiles, and it saddens me—like, how come men wait so long before seeing the doctor?" I shook my head with confusion and went into my office. She then yelled, *"Mr. Ramon will be here at 9:40, and the rest of the day will be light for us."*

Rosalina's referrals started to arrive, so I got right to it. The first two men were perfect for my trial, so I created special files and documented each dosage for the patients to keep a record. There were so many candidates that I had to clear one drawer in my patient file cabinet specifically for those who had been given the 2.0 version. I was tired of men getting away with damaging women—leading them on and leaving them scarred. I had to do something about it, and LH 2.0 was my way.

"Mr. Ramon, head to Room 4. Dr. Hicks will be in soon," Daisy said. *Knock knock.* "Hey, Mr. Ramon, how can I help you?"

I asked. "Doc, I'm not sure what's going on here, but this rash around my penis is burning intensely and itchy." Mr. Ramon's penis looked like he had contracted a nasty infection, so I decided to ask him more questions about his partners.

"Mr. Ramon, have you been in contact with any of the ladies from your past?" I asked him. *"No, only my wife. I was consistent with one lady, but she's in the hospital getting surgery, so it can't be her,"* he replied. *"Ohh no, I see, is she OK? Why is she in the hospital? Her condition could maybe help your case,"* I said to him.

Maybe it was my imagination, but it seemed like he was describing Elana's situation, and I instantly got suspicious. *"Mr. Ramon, give me a second, let me grab soothing cream for your itch and give you something for the burn."* As I walked out of the room, I immediately texted Elana hoping to open up dialogue. "Girl you were on my mind, I hope you are feeling well, I'll be over to see you soon." She then replied, "Hmm yes, I'm doing better. I have two more weeks then I'll be able to get back to work and start living life." "Praise God, … wait, have you heard from Ralpfy the jerk?" I asked. She replied, "Yeah, he texted asking me all sorts of questions about the symptoms I was having before the surgery.

"Girl, apparently he is still experiencing symptoms of some sort, because he told me he's seeing a doctor to help him get straight and he had the nerve to ask me if I'd take him back and forgive him for his mistakes." I interrupted, "No, Bitch!" ….. While the bubble was showing her still typing. I cursed his ass out and I told him to call his wife and leave me the fuck alone," she continued. "Well, I'm glad girl, he's no good," I replied. "Well let me go, I have patients waiting. I'll call you later." "OK I love you," she replied.

As I walked back to Mr., Ramon's room, I felt a burst of anxiety. What am I thinking? Mr. Ramon's first name is Roger. He can't be……., I'd know. I didn't think I could finish his appointment without mentioning Elana just to see whether he knew her, so I wrapped up his visit and grabbed his meds along with a valve of 2.0.

"Mr. Ramon, here is a prescription for the itchiness; it's a soothing cream that minimizes the itch and I'm going to give you another dose of LH vitamin for blood flow. As far as the antibiotics, continue taking them as prescribed and your vitamins for five days then schedule a follow up appointment for 10 days out." "Will do," he replied. Mr. Ramon's condition made him a good candidate to receive LH 2.0, and it was so.

About 2 hours later, my phone started to ring, so I asked Daisy to cover me for me until I was done with my call. "Hello," I said. "What's up, this is Elana and Racquel *they are releasing me today, so no more hospital visits. I know you all had planned to visit, but let's schedule it another time.* " "OK girly," no worries… "I love you and I'll check in with you later, " I said. As I was about to hang up, Daisy called and asked if she could work in the lab. I said yes and since my plans had changed, I'd join her and bring coffee too.

The best answer to anger is SILENCE

~German Proverb~

Weeks had passed and my LH Vitamin had become very popular. I had made tweaks to my serum, and I loved the outcome. Men ED symptoms started to fade, and they were able to hold an erection longer. There were so many follow up appointments on my schedule due to the new version of my serum. In comparison to the original sample, I was getting great reviews. So much so that I presented my ideas to the FDA. Because of my college connections, the approval process got pushed through rather quickly. The administrator approved the drug, but with the disclaimer.

The **FDA** requires disclaimers for supplements, stating that these products have not been evaluated by the FDA and are not intended to diagnose, treat, cure, or prevent any disease.

This disclaimer had to be present on all labels. My clinic was talked about by everyone. Men flooded my entry doors and left several voicemails asking for prescriptions and refills. Their ED symptoms had subsided, and men never felt better. My serum had reached its all-time high. I continued treating men with ED and helped correct their issues despite how I felt about the wrong most men were doing to women. I had surveys sent out to get a census of my product's progress. My ratings were amazing. Regular patients were coming in less, but new referrals were coming in more.

Roselina installed a vending machine in her establishment offering LH Vitamins to all her incoming clients. She made it available to the community by purchasing huge quantities from myself at a lower price and giving her clients one free sample on their visit. Her intakes eventually came to me for ongoing care and prescription refills. My name spread like wildfire, and I was blown away.

*****

I got deals from local clinics, as well as Tal-Mart and even some hospitals that were interested in the Vitamin. After 6 months of my vitamin being offered to the public, I had to open up two more clinics, offering the same service. The demand was so high that our staff went from 12 employees to over 100 employees. We brought on 10 more doctors and more nurses. Daisy became the head nurse, responsible for hiring all nurses, managing interns, and overseeing their placements.

Due to our Saturday workday, Daisy and I became close. One evening, Daisy approached me thanking me for all her successful opportunities and asked if she could shadow me while in the lab. "Let me think about it, maybe Saturdays would be great for training," I said. *"OK,"* she said… *"I can't wait, but I would love to get in the lab."* My eyes popped wide open because having a partner with our LH vitamin would have been great. "Hey, I'm thinking a Saturday shadow in the lab isn't bad at all, let's start next week," I said.

She grabbed her purse and headed to the front desk. I started noticing her doodling pictures of a lab after we spoke, as if she wanted me to know just how bad she wanted to be there. Should I bring her in and accept help with our LH Vitamin? I thought to myself. Am I taking a chance of her finding out about my 2.0 version? Would she report me if she found out? So many questions were going through my head, so I thought No, I think I better keep this to myself and let her shadow me on other projects.

*****

My weekend seemed to fly by, it's already Monday, I thought as I walked into the office. "Good morning, Dr. Hicks, are you ready for the day, Katherine said. I nodded, said good morning, set my cup of Joe down and grabbed my first case. *"Good morning, Doctor Hicks, which room would you like to start with this morning?"* Daisy always asked me the same question knowing my answer never changes. "Room 3 and hey thanks for cleaning the lab after you were done the other night." Her OCD levels were unreal, but that was a quality that I loved. Remembering I had to run and drop off LH VITAMINs to other locations, I asked Daisy if she would call Stephanie, another on-hand nurse, to cover her shifts while she helped me with deliveries. "Absolutely," Daisy said. Being careful not exposed 2.0, I grabbed the clinic's needs for the day and packed them carefully in the trunk of my car.

"Knock knock, I'm doctor Hicks, how are you?" *"I'm OK,"* the gentleman said. "You're new here, looking at his chart, how do you pronounce your name?" *"Rafaeliq, the Q is silent."* "Well, Rafaeliq, with the silent Q, what brings you in today*?"* Rafaeliq had heard about our LH Vitamins and thought it would help him with his blood flow, but after his visit, he was only in need of our daily B-vitamins for energy. "Rafaeliq you look to be just fine, good blood flow, and I'm thinking all you need is an energy boost. Here is a prescription for our B-vitamins, take them once a day and you should feel fine. Not every case that came in warrants our LH Vitamins, but with the reviews, everyone wanted it.' Rafaelq understood and left the clinic feeling better than when he came in.

"Doctor Hicks line one." Daisy said. I rushed to the phone, and it was Mr. Ramon. He was calling from the hospital asking if he can get a prescription for our LH VITAMIN sent to the pharmacy. He was experiencing more burning and itching and thought the hospital could cure that portion while my vitamins helped his ED issue. "Mr. Ramon, are you OK?" I asked. "Not sure Doc, I'm guessing that STD got worse, so I'm here to see about it," he replied. Later that day, Katherine checks her voice mailbox, and it was Mr. Ramon saying the next morning they would be

amputating his penis. His infection was so bad that gangrene started to form on the inside.

*****

Katherine and I sighed with shock, but inside, I was overjoyed. My 2.0 was doing exactly what I intended it to do, to stop men in their tracks but not to the amputation extent. There were several hospital drop offs I needed to handle so after my last patient, I went by Young's hospital and their waiting room was overloaded with aches, pains and moans from men. I could only think that all of this was from my 2.0 serum, but I went on about my day because their pain was their issue.

I dropped off the valves and Facetimed Racquel and Elana. "Hey girlies, what's going on?" *We've missed you, you slut, Racquel said. You stay going MIA on us. We must get together and catch up, "* Elana said. *"Bitch, have you heard the latest?"* Racquel said concerned. "What? There's always something. *I said.* "Bitches sit down," I have some tea. *I was a bit puzzled because my facetime showed me driving. "Girl, can't you see me driving, I am sitting.*

Shaking her head she said *"Elana's ex-man is going through it".* "Wait…why are you telling about Elana, isn't she on the line? I am, Elana said while laughing. You know how much Racquel loves to gossip" we all laughed while Racquel smacked her lips. "What girl, what happened, I said?" I heard from a mutual friend that whatever the condition was that Ralpfy had, it showed up in him differently than his wife.

She had left him after finding out that his penis was infected. It was so bad, it had to be removed. There was talk about her flying him to different states for more opinions, but no one could tell him why this was happening. As Elana was telling me all the man's business, I realized my suspicion about Mr. Ramon being Ralfy was true. He had lied to Elana and given her a fake name. His wife was well-known in their community, so lying to Elana about who he really was helped keep his secret life on the down low. Elana was devastated when she found out that everything, she knew about him was a lie. He got exactly what he deserved. I smiled to myself, because all the connections in the world couldn't get his wife the answers she was looking for. The reason no one could figure out what was happening to him was because my vitamins were blending with all blood types due to the high temperature settings—making detection impossible.

"Jaylee, that bastard is getting exactly what he deserved, why are you quiet?" she asked. "No no no I hear you, that's sad, but guys need to think before they act," I said.

✳✳✳✳✳

We ended the call, and I finished my deliveries. As I pulled up to my last clinic, I noticed 2 detective cars parked in my lot. There weren't any messages or texts that were alarming so it couldn't have anything to do with us. *"Hello Doctor Hicks,"* said Jasmine the receptionist over at the Kingston clinic. "Good morning, Jasmine, what's going on?" *"These detectives stopped by for pamphlet to read up on our LH Vitamins; a friend of theirs referred them to us. LH VITAMIN* Oh ok, welcome, I said. After reading up on our services the detectives scheduled an appointment for labs and their initial visit then thanked us.

Whew, I thought they were here for other reasons I said to myself. There were so many hospital cases where men needed amputations done and I was concerned something may have come back to us. Conviction and fear set it in my heart, so I spent the next two weeks tweaking LH 2.0 to stop the need for amputation as that was never my intent but without success. After a couple of months of this unknown sickness going around, I felt like men were less careless from the conversations we'd have at their appointments, so I stopped administering 2.0 version.

Meanwhile, Elana was getting her life back together and started focusing on herself. With her new outlook on life she spent several weeks at a rejuvenation retreat and came back a new woman. I decided to call her and Racquel to schedule a meeting. Elana's phone rang twice, even though it sometimes took her forever to pick up. *"Hey girl what's up?* Hold on let me add Racquel to the call."* I merged calls and all we heard was, *"Hey bitch!"* "Let's get together tonight for dinner and drinks, are y'all in," I said. *"Hell Yeah,"* they both answered. "OK cool let's get together around 8:00pm. Racquel, I'll grab you first then Elana, I'll pick you up afterwards. Right as we were ending the call my other line beeped, "Hello?" *"Hey, this is Daisy, I need to talk to you,"* *she said nervously.*

"What's up girly, are you OK?" I asked. *"Jaylee, I've always been honest with you so I'm not going to stop now…"* I instantly got nervous, "Just blurt it out," I said. Daisy had been busy lately and a bit distracted. Well, on this day, she saw 6 patients from two of our other locations in Dominion Heights. Work had gotten a bit overwhelming, but her commitment to getting the job done always came first. Daisy was asked to consult on a patient who had several allergy restrictions in their file. She was sure that the medication Nurse Gwen suggested wouldn't interfere with his current meds, only it did. "Mr. Dubey went into anaphylactic shock and almost passed away. This mistake put Gwen in a panic. They called the ambulance and rushed Mr. Dubey to the local hospital. He was admitted and released, but he had threatened to sue our clinic and the threat scared Daisy.

*****

Jaylee, I swear I didn't see he was allergic to aspirin. It wasn't in his file; I looked thoroughly and so did Gwen, Daisy expressed. As she was telling me the story, I went over to the clinic and pulled up the company's file where all patients from all clinics were stored. Mr. Dubey's file did not have a warning label saying he was allergic to aspirin. Daisy was correct, he never told us about his allergies, even though the question is listed seven different ways on our forms. "OK Daisy, meet me at Dominion Heights hospital, let's go have a chat." *"OK Doctor Hicks, I'll be there in 5."* Daisy and I met at the hospital where we chatted with Mr. Dubey about his condition, he calmed down and agreed to listen to how the mistake could've happened.

We showed him his intake papers, proving that there were no allergies listed in his file. He apologized for his mistake and decided to drop the threat of suit but under one condition. He wanted us to prescribe him our LH Vitamin and to be seen at our Bridgetown clinic for future care. I grabbed his hand and said "absolutely". Mr. Dubey was excited to try our vitamins for the first time and was relieved that he was OK after his scare. Daisy sighed with relief. She couldn't stop thanking me for not firing her and that the mistake she had made, she'd never do again. Normally, Daisy would dig deep before signing off on anything, but because of that day's rush, she trusted Gwen. I asked her to sit and told her everything was ok and asked that she be more careful when signing off on medication.

Elana and Racquel had called several times and as usual, I sent their calls to voicemail. I had no energy to argue with Racquel from not answering, so I decided to text them both, tell them what happened then ask for their forgiveness for canceling. I headed to Royal's Chinese Buffet to grab myself dinner since I missed the meet with the girls. At this point, I was exhausted and wanted to relax. I couldn't help but notice the look on Daisy's face; she still looked bothered, so I invited her over for Chinese. She looked shocked because I had never extended her an invitation; however, her sadness got the best of me. *"Yes, Doctor Hicks," she said, "I'd love to come."* "Daisy, please call me Jaylee, working hours are over, I said"

We ordered egg Foo young, grabbed a nice bottle of wine and decided to watch movies. All night, she kept revisiting the incident from earlier, so I decided to show her my mini lab in the backroom to get her mind off things. She was so excited, she left her food, grabbed her wine and made herself comfortable. *"Wow, Jaylee, I could spend all night in here!"* she said.

*****

We laughed; she looked around more then went back to watch TV. Daisy looked around my home and said *"Jaylee, can I ask you a personal question?"* *"Absolutely,"* I said nervously. *"Are you seeing anyone?"* she asked. I grabbed the wine to fill up our cups and said, "No, not at the current time. What about you?" I asked. She walked over to me and said, *"No there's no one, work comes first."* We laughed, drank more wine and eventually fell asleep on the couch. What seemed like 20 minutes of sleep was actually hours then that damn alarm sounded wake up, wake up, wake up, wake up, wake up.

"Hey Daisy, it's time to get up!". *Dang girl, we drank all that wine, and I didn't even think of calling an Uber last night.* "Girl that's OK, just go in my closet and grab something to wear, I'm sure it's something in there that you can fit. Daisy didn't seem ok with that so she asked if I could drop her off at home on our way to the office. I said yes, jumped in the shower, grabbed my coffee with avocado toast and we headed to work.

"Good morning, Doctor Hicks," Katherine said. *"How was your night last night?"* she asked. "I'm sure you heard about the hospital scare with Mr. Dubey?" *"Yes, I did,"* Katherine said… *"So, how'd it go?"* she asked. "I grabbed his file from the company's database, and he had never listed his allergies, he agreed the error was a mistake and ask to try our LH VITAMIN. He also wanted a visit at this location from now on, so I'd be his ongoing care physician." *"Ohh good, so what did you do with Daisy? She's great and never really made mistakes,"* she said. *"Well of course I got on her and explained how she could have done better, but she was nervous, which she thought she'd be fired over."* We both chuckle and say, *"Never!"*

"Today is light, no calls from Roselina, only vitamin refills," Katherine said. "Ohh great, I'd probably get to go home early. *"I'm going to call over to the other clinics to confirm their stock and if all goes well, we'll be out at 12,"* Katherine said. We slapped hands and greeted Daisy as she was walking into the office. Daisy lived two blocks from the clinic, so it didn't take her long to get to the office. "Good morning girly, set up room three for me," I said. *"OK, it will be ready in 10 minutes,"* Daisy said.

*****

Katherine leaned over to Daisy and said, *"I hope you know how valuable you are and you're a huge asset here.* Daisy eyes watered while saying *"Oh my, I'm so happy to hear that, Katherine. I love it here and I would never want to jeopardize this place.* Daisy gave us both a hug of thanks, then Katherine informed her to let us know if there is ever a time she's in need of help. She expressed how much we needed her around here, so she said she would reach out to our hiring department and get some part timers to help out. Daisy thanked us and went to prepare room three.

"Hold on, this is all we have today?" Daisy said. *"Yes, we're getting out of here at 12:00pm." "Great!" she shouted. I headed to see my first patient and the rest of the day flew by. I updated my charts then started feeling tired. How much longer? I thought. "Doctor Hicks, how about lunch?" Daisy asked. "Girl I'll eat when I get home, all I want to do is chill in front of the TV because I'm tapped out." "Ohh OK, I feel you. Well get some rest, I think I'm going to grab steak and potatoes and chill too." "Steak and potato sound yummy but I was exhausted and knew I wouldn't want to stop.*

Two hours later, Daisy said to me, *"Room 4 is waiting and that's your last patient."* I was so excited to get home. I finished up my last room, locked my office and were all set to leave. I was going to call the girls, but I wanted to relax, so I figured a shake for dinner, a little TV then off to sleep I go. We all left the office and went our separate ways. As I pulled up to my garage, I instantly felt hungry for food. I thought a shake would be nice, but I knew later I would be hungry and would be too lazy to go back out. I tossed my mail on the counter, put away my purse, turned my TV on and ran water for quick shower to get comfortable.

Mr. Bean (my plush pillow) was calling my name. I love snuggling with Mr. Bean, so after my shower, I grabbed him off on the couch and snuggled tight. I must have been asleep for a while, because when the doorbell rang, the movie I was watching had ended. "Yes, who is it?" I asked, *"It's me, Daisy, can I come up?"* "Yes, I'll tell the doorman to let you up." I was concerned because she had not called and last night wasn't supposed to turn into an every night thing.

*****

"Sorry Jaylee, I decided to bring you dinner, it's my way of saying thanks. You left the office looking exhausted because of me, so I wanted to help you by providing dinner." "Ohh my, thanks Daisy. Come in, let's have dinner together, I mean you're already here." We started to binge watch Grey's Anatomy and because we were so full, we both fell asleep again. There was a loud sound coming from the TV that woke me up so I nudged Daisy to wake her, but she didn't move. *"Daisy, we both fell asleep, it's time to get up."* She looked so tired, so I invited her to stay again. I really

didn't mind the company; it had been a while since I had anyone stay over. She thanked me again and asked if I was sure she could stay.

I assured her that it was no problem and that I enjoyed her company. As she walked towards the guest room, she turned and looked at me and said, *"Jaylee, I'd like to show you something."* I walked towards the guest room with her and before I entered the room, she had turned around and planted a big kiss right on my lips. "I'm so sorry Jaylee, I'm so sorry," she said apologetically. I was shocked, not so much at her, but that I allowed it. I didn't know what to make of it. I had experienced women in college, but I never thought I'd have a full relationship with one. Daisy was just my type, now that I thought about it. She was caring, intelligent, Mexican and black, curly short hair, with a beautiful body but I never looked at her in that way, so I was surprised.

It was clear she wanted more; my only hesitation would be that I was her boss. I couldn't entertain that; what would the staff think, what would Katherine say? Yeah, this is a bad idea I thought to myself. *"Daisy, no need to apologize." I said.* As I went to exit her room, she turned me around to face her. She ran her fingers through my hair and said you're the most beautiful woman I ever seen, she removed her top, pulled me in close to her then removed mine. I was speechless but turned on by her dominance. Her clothes were off at this point, and we made love right on the couch. I was so used to being in charge at work that her being in charge in the bedroom was attractive, I don't know, I think that made her more appealing. She was so romantic, soft and gentle. She took her time with me, made sure I was comfortable, then asked me if I wanted her to stay. Of course, I said yes, there was no way I was letting this mamacita go.

Daisy left to grab clothes from her house and hurried back to me. I was shocked, maybe a little surprised about how I felt, but happy. I showered again, put away our leftover food, then started to think what it would be like to be with her. Would others understand?

*****

How upset would Katherine be? Would the clinic demand a transfer? All these things came to mind as I waited for Daisy to return. There was soft music playing in the background, candles lit and when Daisy entered the front door, she grabbed my hands then led me to the bedroom. We knew we would have to further discuss this arrangement, but we couldn't keep our hands off one another. Sex was amazing. We fell asleep in each other's arms and to be honest, I had never felt so safe. Two weeks into our relationship, Daisy went to work at our dominion clinic after filing our relationship papers with HR. Surprisingly, Katherine was on board. She was heavy in her religion, but she never judged anyone. She'd always say *"I'm gonna pray for you."* We were safe with her. I just never wanted to disappoint Katherine.

Our business was really taking off. Patients' census forms started coming in heavy but since Mr. Jamerson was due to come back into the office, he was bringing his census form with him. "Doctor Hicks, I'll get Mr. Jamerson set up in room 3," said Betty. *"OK thanks, let's get the others going while we wait for him."*

Beep, beep there was a medical release form report being requested through our fax line. Mr. Jamerson had requested his records to be faxed to Laney Lane hospital. I couldn't help but wonder what this request was, but due to HIPAA, they couldn't disclose. Jessica, our administrator, gathered his records and sent them over. *"Doctor Hicks, you can scratch Mr. Jamerson off today's schedule, he won't be coming in today." "I figured,"* I said, and I continued to work.

It was 4:45 PM and I was just about to clean up when suddenly, our follow-up inbox filled quickly. Each clinic was filled with follow-up appointments. There were so many appointments that we started scheduling them the very next morning. Most of them I had recognized; the others seemed to be new patients, which was weird because they chose "follow up" option on their forms. I had a good tracking system for all those who I had given 2.0 to, so I was ready to hear the bad news of the need for amputation.

*****

I put everyone on the schedule then texted Daisy saying, "I'm headed home." Daisy had agreed to meet with me at the house but wanted to stop by the office lab first. She was so obsessed with the lab, so I agreed and told her that I'll see her once she got home. I didn't realize it would be four hours later when she called to say, *'I'm on my way.'* I was upset, because I really wanted to be with her, but I quickly got over it after she texted that she was almost home. I heard the door opening and from the look on her face she seemed exhausted. Babe, are you ok? You look tired. "I am" she said and tomorrow will be worse there are so many appointments scheduled. I looked over at her and said *"Yeah, that's how our*

Bridgetown location is too." I had scheduled them out equally so that there wouldn't be a single clinic overwhelmed with patients. We discussed our day, had dinner and went to bed.

I really enjoyed how the relationship was going. We respected one another's space, started learning each other's habits and we both were passionate about the medical field. Surprisingly, we have a similar history regarding youth trauma and made a mutual decision to seek therapy both individually, then together. That would be the only way we would work. As I laid down, I couldn't help but think about my past and how much I'd been through. Our relationship was still new, there was no way I was going to share everything with Daisy, not at the present time, she'd run away I thought.

So many questions came to mind, I knew if I didn't shut my mind off, I'd never get any rest, so I said my prayers and went to sleep.

Wake up, wake up, wake up, that damn alarm again. *"Babe, you have to change that alarm, it scares me every morning,"* Daisy said. I chuckled then headed to shower. My mornings were the exact same, except now I'm waken by a gorgeous Latina who seemed to be falling in love with showering. "Daisy please, we have to get to work early so don't start anything." She assured me she only needed 10 minutes, but it always lasted longer. We'd make love in the shower again and again and again, both leaving home exhausted.

To love and be loved is to feel the sun from both sides

~David Scott~

Chapter 4

"*Good morning, Betty. How are you liking Saturday workdays?*" "*Actually, I enjoy the quietness, and I can get more done in preparation for the upcoming week.*" *I know what you mean, Im glad you like it well start me with room 7,*" I said. At first, I started to panic from the scheduling list but then there were only 5 who needed a full check up all the others were there because they needed copies of their medical records. Men had started to seek out specialists for their condition which made me worry but because my serum was undetectable, I felt safe.

Each clinic's records were current and up to date. There weren't any red flags to worry about, but most of our files included over 400 men who experienced amputation. I carried on with caution and destroyed all traces of our 2.0 version. Men we're being more careful, and our LH Vitamin was provided everywhere. More men we're coming into the clinic for annual visits and actually kept up with their follow up appointments.

I've never seen such a high volume of cases. It's as if they had been warned and knew they needed to be more careful now than ever. I decided to promote more of our male care packages that included 30-day male birth control, our famous LH vitamin, and our B-vitamins for energy. They were all safe to take together so I worried less, and the community loved it more. I couldn't be prouder of myself.

Two weeks passed and Racquel's birthday was approaching. Daisy and I had already confirmed our appearance, so we got up early that Saturday morning, headed to our hair appointments then got facials. This would be the first time the girls saw Daisy face to face, as they had only spoken on the phone. She was excited and wanted to look her best. We finished up our errands, hurried home to dress and made our way to Racquel's house.

*****

Daisy was a bit nervous about house parties after her rape experience at her uncle's home when she was younger. *"Babe don't worry, you'll be safe. I'm with you,"* I said to calm her nerves. As we pulled up to Racquel's house, there were four guys on the porch playing Dominoes. *"What's up doc?"* (mocking roger rabbit the cartoon character). *"Hey y'all how's it going?"* We all laughed because it was an inside joke that we told each other, but Daisy didn't understand it. *"Let's go inside Babe,"* I grabbed her hand and headed to Racquel's kitchen. *"What's up chick?"* *"Hey Daisy,"* Racquel said. *"Happy birthday!"* Daisy said while holding 2 bottles of Racquel's favorite wine. Racquel hugged Daisy so tight, it looked as if she didn't want to let her go.

"Where's Elana?" I asked. *"She's up front."* We followed Racquel to the front and grabbed the seat. Elana was playing spades, and we could tell she was winning from all her foul language and the way she was slapping the cards on the table. *"Hey bitch,"* Elana said. Daisy looked confused, so I explained to her she was harmless, and this is just how we greeted each other. Daisy looked at me and said, *"Yeah I'm gonna love y'all."* Daisy started to feel comfortable, not surprising, because Racquel always made sure everyone felt right at home.

Hours had passed by and my baby was drunk. Not so much that she couldn't stand, just drunk enough to express her sexual needs that she wanted from me. She whispered that she was going to help Racquel clean then we were going home; I knew at that point, she wanted another shower experience. I decided I'd wait to be sure that I was sober enough to drive home. While waiting, I overheard friends of Racquel talking about one of their mutual friends and the situation they were in. Some guys they grew up with were in the hospital due to a STD and now they were getting their penis cut off (in their words).

"What?" One girl said. *"Yeah, girl everyone is talking about it; it's all-over social media. I bet these guys will start strapping*

up now," she said. *"I heard one guy got an attorney because he was thinking to sue the girl who he thinks gave him the STD."* As they were talking, I got concerned. *Is this person really going to sue someone for getting an STD? Could this really be true?* Daisy walked towards me, and I told her, *"Baby let's go."*

*****

She tried telling me they had almost finished cleaning, but I was ready to go. I left nervously, so much so that I didn't say goodbye to the girls I just sent them a text and told them I wasn't feeling well. Daisy made her advances once we got home, but I was so distracted over the conversation I had heard that I couldn't perform. I set my alarm to get up earlier than usual so that I could go to the lab alone. The next day, while Daisy was still asleep, I creeped out the bed and got dressed... I knew I'd have to explain my disappearance, so I made sure to bring back burritos from her favorite restaurant.

Once I got to the clinic, I started looking at more samples, but I couldn't find any inconsistencies, any trace that would detect our 2.0 version. *Why am I so nervous?* I ask myself. I guess it's my conscience I never wanted men to lose their male parts I only wanted it to sting a little... I grabbed the food, headed home and spent the rest of the day with my love.

Morning came so fast and all I heard was that damn alarm I didn't want to get up, so I asked Daisy if she could turn it off. Exhaustion had set in. She reached over, stopped the alarm and kissed me good morning. Traffic was a bit different this day, and Daisy decided to go to the Bridgetown location and help out.

"Good morning, Katherine, how's it going?" I said, while handing her a cup of coffee from my favorite place. *"Everything is good, but we were served a summons for patients' medical records. Apparently, there is a patient who's suing his girl for giving him a STD and trauma. His lawyer is requesting his medical records from us. They are stating our findings could be biased, so they're getting reviewed by another physician"* Katherine said.

*****

"Do you know what this is about?" Katherine asked me while surfing the internet. *"No, I don't, but I'll get it pulled up and sent over right away. I don't want any legal issues.* I gathered his file, gave it to Jessie, asked her to make a copy and FedEx it to their attorney. *"Start me with room 3 Betty,"* I said as I walked towards my office. Daisy had left 30 minutes before me today, which was weird, seeing that we were going right home after work.

I decided to text her when I was done, so I grabbed my phone and said, *"Babe, I'm all done, I'm about to head home."* I chatted with Katherine as I waited for a response, but nothing. Katherine was so chatty today, because she had set a meeting with financial advisors to discuss her finances and her ability to start a new venture. *"You're awful happy today,"* I said, *"What's going on?"* *"Jaylee, have a seat, we need to talk."*

I didn't know which end of the field she was coming from, so I sat down, and I said, "Girl, you are scaring me. What's up?" She looked at me and said, *"I'm opening my own church. I've decided to promote Stephanie the receptionist and devote 100% of my time building a church home."* It was a bittersweet moment, because our business had expanded and for all that Katherine does it would have been too hard to keep up with. *"Congratulations Katherine, I said sadly."*

Katherine knew I'd suffer panic attacks, so before I got worked up, she said *"I got attorneys to cover us for any legal issues. I created a Trust for portions of our assets so that they stay safe. We have overseas accounts investments that's under trust numbers so that if anything happens, we're covered and would never have to work again."* I started to feel better because while she was getting her finances together, she was handling mines as well. Katherine is the one who keeps me together so the thought of losing her felt like I was losing a piece of myself.

*****

"Our money is working for us," she said. *"I have asked our accountant that we've always used to continue where I left off and I'll be reviewing all transactions, purchases and ledgers every month, so I'm not completely out of it."* She reminded me how well we were doing but that her talents were needed elsewhere. I was sad, but I understood the clinic was my baby; she helped me to create something beautiful, so I wished her all the luck in opening her church. I later became one of her members even though I'd watch it online most of the time.

She reminded me how confident she was in letting Stephanie handle the day-to-day and I was comfortable as well. We promoted our staff accordingly and always gave credit where it was due. I looked at my watch and two hours had passed without a text back from Daisy. *"OK Katherine, I'm heading out,"* I said. Katherine followed me out and we went our separate ways. As I was driving home, I couldn't help but think *Wow, we have two more weeks with Katherine.*

I felt a vibration come from my pocket; it was a text from Daisy, *"Baby where are you?"* Because I was driving, I didn't text back, so I called her, *"Where are you?"* I asked. *"Sorry, I was in the groove and didn't hear my phone. I had my head planted to the scope; I'm just in love with this lab. I'm gone grab dinner and meet you at home."* As I pulled into the garage, I noticed Daisy had not got there, so I rushed in, lit candles, set the table and turned the television on.

Breaking news coming from channel 13, another update on this dreadful disease that's effecting men. *14 more men have come forward after the ongoing lawsuit to a woman who spread such a horrible disease, it caused men to have their penises removed. The 14 men had no relationship to the woman, but all the men had the same STD.* I turned the volume up as the local hospitals' president spoke. He said," "Our hospital has seen and treated several cases over the last week, and it is getting worse.

*****

"We're still investigating and will keep the public updated on this breakout. We plan to dig deep into this, as we brought on Doctor JS Simpson from the Georgia outward community center to help with the investigation." My eyes popped up because I had heard about him. He's a very prominent Dr. in Georgia with an enormous tech lab. *"Babe, I'm home,"* Daisy said. I grabbed the bottle of wine and poured out the biggest glass I could find. *"Babe*

what's wrong why are you drinking it that way?" "No reason, let's eat." From the look on her face, I could tell she knew something was bothering me, but she stood quiet.

The rest of our work week went smoothly. We were preparing for Katherine's new venture and discussing new office rules. Stephanie had really stepped up into her new role. My schedule was well put together and timed perfectly, almost better than Katherine. Stephanie played no games when it came to promptness, it's almost like she knew one day she'd be in control. She created an auto text app, which allowed patients to confirm their visits. If a patient needed to keep or reschedule their appointment, they would have to text us two hours beforehand or else there would be a $50 fee.

This new way of scheduling allowed the clinic to run smoothly and effectively. Our time never ran over and there were times we were all able to help with other clinics, because patients utilized the text app as they should. The text app was so successful, we implemented it over all the clinics and everyone was pleased. About two weeks with Katherine gone, the office was running well and everyone felt like nothing had changed, but of course, we missed her. *"Good morning, how can I help you?"* Stephanie said. *"Is Doctor Hicks in?"* A sheriff with a bright orange jacket stepped to the front desk and Stephanie said, *"No she's not." "I have an urgent packet for her, can you sign accepting it on her behalf?* he said, so she signed it, and waited for me to arrive.

"Good morning, Renee, how's it going today?" I asked, just as I did every morning. *"Our load is manageable, everyone confirmed their appointments for today, so I started you with room*

three." I laugh, because she always tried doing the nurse's job, giving me rooms. *"Wait Doctor Hicks, before you go in the back, here's an envelope."*

I took the envelope and headed to the back, *"Thank you,"* I said, thinking maybe these were labs, but to my surprise, it was a summons to appear in court. I was nervous and I couldn't hold it together, so I panicked and called Daisy. She tried calming me, but it didn't help, so she said she would come over. I was so distracted I asked Dr. Chui to cover the rest of my appointments. By the time Daisy had finished her last patient and got here, I was sitting in the car, shaking. "Babe, what's wrong?" she asked. *"I have been summoned to court." "For what?"* She said. *"One of our patients is suing his ex-girlfriend for spreading a disease that caused him to have to amputate his penis."*

She looked confused, like what did that have to do with us. *"So..."* she said, *"why do you have to appear?" "Because I was the attending doctor, they want files on all the patients involved to compare records."* Daisy never stopped asking questions, so the more she asked, the more I felt I needed to tell her. *"Baby, relax, just give them the records and you'll be done,"* she said. I agreed and we went home. The next day, I sent over all the patients' records to Doctor Simpson, hoping he couldn't find anything that could tie it back to us.

Two months passed, and I got a call that there was going to be a deposition coming up, so they needed to go over a couple of things with me before then. The sheriff had asked me to come to the police station early that Monday morning; he had a few questions, but to my surprise, Doctor Simpson was there as well.

"Good morning, I'm Doctor Hicks, I'm here for a scheduled meeting with the sheriff." They led me to the question room and asked me to wait. As I waited, Elana Racquel and Katherine were texting. Katherine had been blowing up my phone for weeks leading up to that I just couldn't come to terms with telling her about my involvement. *"Girl, are you OK? Daisy called us saying you were at the police station,"* they said. So, I texted them back before the questioning started and told them I'd explain later.

*****

The Sherriff and detective questioning went on for hours, so I asked, "Am I suspect?" The detective said they were questioning all who were connected to the victims and said they were at the process of elimination point, only it felt different to me. They had Dr. Simpson in the next room, so they would leave then come back to me, as if he was feeding them questions to ask me. The final question that brought everything to a halt was, *"We're going to need a sample of your LH Vitamin for this investigation to clear you from any liability."* I asked, *"Why and do I need an attorney?"* He said, *"No, but the defendant stated that you were his primary physician just as those other men had. We're just trying to remove you and your clinic from further questioning."*

I told them I wanted to consult an attorney and get back to them. I'm guessing they were prepared for my response because they already had a warrant in place to search my lab. *I bet that's why Daisy and Katherine were calling, wondering why the police were there going through files*, I said to myself. I contacted my attorney, who advised me to cooperate to clear my name. Thankfully, nothing was left there, incriminating like I thought, they took a sample of our LH VITAMIN, and they dusted the scope at my workstation. Dr. Simpson had reviewed the valves taken from my lab to see if there were a correlation between the men symptoms and what I prescribed them. He then noticed a chemo serum kit that was picked up during the search and labeled it to review later.

Mistakes were made.
Others were blamed.

~Darynda Jones~

Chapter **5**

ourt was scheduled for next Wednesday at 8:00am and because it was such a public case, they aired portions of it on the 10:00 o'clock news. I followed the case, because Dr. P-body clinic was mentioned and I thought this would destroy our name, but with the success of our LH Vitamins, it made our name more popular. The case went on for months and our clinics grew larger. Daisy and I started delegating work and spending more time together. We spent less time in the clinic, giving each employee room to grow. I remember the day we decided to let the staff run the office day-to-day; that was the day I proposed to her.

She was so excited, she had given me a date that was already set in her mind early on that I'd remember.

Daisy always assured me that no matter what, she'd always be there for me and would never give up on me. I loved her loyalty and her values when it came to relationships. She often talked about having children and with the new technology, I was going to make it happen. Daisy was my everything; I couldn't imagine life without her. I made promises and I was going to keep them. She deserved the world. Her heart was pure, she was kind, and she loved people.

One morning, two sheriffs came to our home banging on our door. They were yelling, *"Open up, we're here for Doctor Hicks."* Daisy opened the door and asked them to wait. As I walked out of our bedroom, they said to me, *"Doctor Hicks, you have the right to remain silent."* I was under arrest for manslaughter. I couldn't believe it, so I told Daisy to call our attorney. Daisy screamed and cried saying, *"No please don't take her!"* I lowered my head and dropped a tear. My thoughts from the start never included a love life. I selfishly committed a crime that ruined the very thing I've always wanted, and that was love.

*****

I've thought about all the what ifs. I thought about Daisy being in the arms of another woman, about our late-night talks regarding adopting children. I also thought about how my actions had ruined so many lives. I built my clinic on integrity and somewhere along the line, I lost my own. Officer Jefferson grabbed my arms, got his cuffs and arrested me right in my living room. *"Baby,"* Daisy said,

"I'm calling our attorney right now and I'll be right behind you. Don't you hurt her," she said, *"I love you Baby."* Daisy's phone rang right as we were leaving, "Hello?" She said with an attitude. *"Hey girl, it's Elana, ... I was just checking on our girl. How is she?"*

"She's being arrested as we speak, and I don't know what to do. I'll call y'all back, I need to contact our attorney." Daisy ended the call and got in touch with attorney Davis. He was keen for no nonsense in the courtroom, very expensive, but worth it. When she finally got in touch with him, they both headed to the police station, ready to plead my case. The jail was cold, the officers were unconcerned, and I thought, *could this be the end? Could they have put the pieces together? Doctor Simpson was a great forensics Dr. and science was his specialty; they had called him in as an expert witness due to the many amputation cases he had reviewed from the items he retrieved from the warrant.*

"Jaylee, your attorney is here," Officer Jefferson said. *"Hi Jaylee, Daisy called, she's in the lobby. She let me know you're in here, what's going on?"* the attorney said. *"They arrested me for conspiracy to commit a crime. They're saying medical negligence and mentioned malpractice suit. Apparently, there is a man who's suing his ex-girlfriend for knowingly spreading an STD. From what I know, their symptoms were so bad amputation was needed."* *"OK, but how does that involve you?"* He said. *"All the men involved were once treated at my clinic."* I tried to explain how popular my LH Vitamin had become, so most men came on their own after being referred to our clinic. *"My clinic was known for Ed correction, but we provided male medical care as well.*

*****

"I'm guessing they're thinking it was something negligent or intentional that happened on my watch." "OK I'm going to call the officer in; only answer what I tell you to. I'm going to get you bonded out on ROR, because you're a respectable doctor who has never committed a crime." "Officer Jefferson, can you please come in here?" "Yes, I'd like to ask your client a couple of questions," the officer said. *"What kind of questions?* My attorney asked. *"Did your client prescribe LH Vitamins to each of the men involved?"* My attorney jumped in, *"Wait what does that have to do with anything? She's a physician."*

"Well, it's being said something had to be prescribed to men to create this kind of urgency." "Yes, I was their physician, I was their primary care physician." "OK my next question is, why did you have chemo kits in your lab?" My attorney immediately said, *"Where did you get that from? Did you have a warrant and what did it cover?" "Yes, we had a warrant for LH Vitamins.* Officer Jefferson leaned over to me and said, *"Jaylee we're trying to get to the bottom of this, we just want the facts, why did you have those kits in your lab?"*

Attorney Davis jumped right in and said, *"Your warrant only covered the LH Vitamins. Wanting to know why she had other items in her lab; it is none of your business. She doesn't have to answer that. Did you receive the LH vitamin?"* "Yes," Officer Jefferson said. *"Then that's all you need."* My attorney drilled the officer until they gave up. I was released on my own recognizance but was given a court date two weeks out.

"Babe, you're out," Daisy said, "I've missed you so much." She was acting as if I was gone for years. "Thanks Babe, I missed you too," I said. My attorney scheduled a meeting for us sometime that week to build our case and that's when my life started to crumble.

*****

Later that day, my phone rang, and it was Katherine. *What do I say? She's going to be so disappointed as I almost ruined the business. "Hello?" "Ohh my girl, are you OK?"* she asked. *"Yes, I am, they held me for some questions, because of those men who needed those surgeries and that lawsuit. I'm drained, but we need to meet so let's have coffee and I'll fill you in.* Katherine was like a sister to me; I couldn't lie to her. She trusted me with so much, as I her. She probably be pissed but she will never leave me nor give up on me, especially after she hears the entire truth. The advantage was, Katherine could not speak on anything I told her due to religion confidentiality. I respect Katherine and her cloth, but I needed to explain myself.

I decided to go into the office that next morning with a positive attitude despite what went down. *"Good morning, Doctor Hicks." "Good morning, Betty. I'm so sorry to have scared you, please forgive me."* Betty replied, *"One thing you better know about me, is if you're rocking, I'm rolling."* Betty was always faithful and loyal; this was the number one reason I was open with the staff, because in times of trouble, they're always going to be there. *"Jaylee,"* Betty said, *"No matter what's going on, I got your back. Doctor P-Body Clinic will live on and I'm going to do all that I can to see that your name stays intact."*

"I love you Girly and I appreciate your loyalty," I said. I hugged her then asked that she scheduled an employee meeting for two weeks out on a Monday. I didn't know how I was going to break the news. I decided to rehearse it over and over in my head all the way up until the next day. On my ride home from the office, I sat in the garage and cried. I cried because my plans were thought out so well, I never thought I'd be facing this, as I was so careful.

*****

I put the keys in the door, walked inside and to my surprise, Elana and Racquel were there for support. My girls always came through for me. They hugged me and just like that, we were all crying. Daisy walked over to me and said, *"Baby stop it, don't cry."* I was shocked that they were there, so I asked what's going on, *"Why y'all here?"* *"Bitch, to see you,"* Racquel said. *"I'm here because I was summoned in your case,"* Elana said. *"What? Why were you summoned?"* I asked. *"Because the guy I was telling y'all about, Ralpfy, Stephen, Jake whatever he wants to call himself, he decided to get in on the suit too."* My heart started to race because before she got too far into her story, I thought everyone had banded together to attack me.

And just like Elana, she cursed him out and said, *"Bastard, I don't have anything to give, so sue me if you want to,"* and we all chuckled. My stomach felt weird because I knew they were getting close and I'd be exposed soon.

Daisy had bought food, so we ate, and watched movies then chatted a bit more. *"OK bitch, I'm heading home,"* it was getting late, so they grabbed their things and left. *"I'll keep you all posted,"* I said as they walked out the door. *"Yes, keep us posted and I'll keep you posted on this dumb summons I just received.; that man lost his damn mind trying to sue me."* I watched them leave then locked the door.

Daisy had made sure everyone was gone and decided to run me bath water" "I'll be with you in a minute she said." The house smelled amazing, Daisy cleaned like she always did, sprayed freshener and vacuumed the rug once everyone left. She set the alarm then joined me for a bath. *"I love you Daisy so much,"* I said. *"I love you more,"* she said. We laid in bed, snuggled and fell asleep. Friday came so quickly; I was anxious and full of anxiety as I headed to the attorney's office for our initial meeting. I stopped and grabbed more coffee, because I had finished the cup that I had brewed that morning.

*****

As I pulled up to the attorney's office, I rang the bell to be let into their gated community. *"Hi, my name is Jaylee, and I have an appointment with attorney Davis." "Yes, come on up,"* the lady said through the intercom. As I drove up the long trail, I said to myself, *I'm in the wrong profession.* A lady with a two-piece suit was at the door to greet me, standing between their French glass doors to what looked to be a palace. *"Good morning, Doctor Hicks, let's get settled."* I was amazed, because here I am in this beautiful office and out comes this beautiful black woman, who I could only imagine was a no-nonsense attorney, Miss Stephanie Lenox.

"I can tell by the look on your face you were expecting attorney Davis. "My apologies, he had been summoned to a pending trial in Italy, so he referred you to me as I am his partner. I am familiar with your case, so there's no need to be concerned." She was breathtaking; she walked softly, but with confidence. Her smile gleamed with joy and while I may be facing charges, I'm here thinking of ways to make her mine. *"Dr. Hicks are you OK?"* she said. *"Ohh yes, I'm OK, your office is beautiful. I don't remember it looking this way,"* I said as I followed her to the next room. *"Yeah, attorney Davis renovated this place, and he moved to our location on the hill. This belongs to me,"* she said with cockiness.

We chatted for a while, and she made me comfortable. Then she popped the question, *"Is there any merit?"* *"No, I'm confused as to why I'm involved when the guy who started this ordeal is suing girlfriend."* *"Well, they brought in Dr. Simpson an amazing trial scientist who brought up the question regarding the similarities between all the men. The common denominator was you."* I started to panic at that point. I didn't know if she was there for me or working for the other side. She walked behind her big black desk and said to me, *"First I need you to sign this disclaimer, then you'll receive more paperwork via FedEx. You'll bring those papers completed at our next meet."* I wondered why FedEx was her shipping choice when I was right there. She must have read my mind because she said, *"The Internet is fine, but I want no chances of hacks, so FedEx is how you receive documents from me."*

*****

"I will prepare all your paperwork, investigate everything that they have and present it to you for review. I do not like to lose,

so at our next meet, I'm going to ask you some real difficult questions and I want you to spill the beans, good, bad or ugly. Oh, and I'll need one of your LH Vitamin samples to give to our own lab to investigate ASAP. Here's my card, grab you some coffee and I'll see you at our next meet." She was cold and to the point; I'm sure I had questions, but suddenly, everything went blank. I think I was attracted to her cockiness and confidence, two major characteristics that I love. She shook my hand, and I left.

The entire ride home, I struggled with myself. *Should I or should I not say something? Her record was impeccable; she'll find out and the first thing she'll say is 'why did you lie to me?' 'I can fix anything, just don't lie.'* I'm sure that's what she'll say if she finds out from the opposing attorney. I took the rest of the day off, because Doctor Chui covered my patients that day. I called Daisy to give her an update, and my baby was busy as usual, handling business at every location. *She's going to be my wife,* I thought to myself, but *wait a minute, Where's my head? I just had dirty thoughts about Attorney Stephanie. No, I'm not going to ruin what Daisy, and I built, she's my baby, and I love her* I thought to myself.

"Siri call baby," I said. *Hey, I'm glad you called, how'd your meet go?"* Daisy said. *"It went well and her office..."* Before I could finish my sentence, jealous Daisy came out and said, *"Her? "What happened to Attorney Davis?"* I chuckled and said, *"Babe, he was summoned to another international case, so he referred my case to her, she's, his partner."* Daisy wasn't hearing anything; all she kept saying was, *"I have to meet her."* I began again, *"Babe the office was beautiful..."* She interrupted me and said, *"I'll see*

you when you get home." She sounded frustrated, so we ended the call.

*****

Never make a Latina woman angry I thought so I bought some rose petals, and decided to decorate our room, had bath water ready, wine and dinner ready for when she got home. I thought to myself *all of this and I didn't even do anything.* When Daisy got home, the look on her face was scary. She pulled off her scrubs, grabbed my hand and we made love. *Wow, is that what jealousy does?* I reminded her that she was all I wanted and all I needed, and she didn't have to be jealous of anyone. The rest of that night went amazing; it was like a dream. I can't say for sure if we finished our food, but I was left satisfied.

The alarm sounded so we got dressed and headed to the office. Today was our scheduled office meeting and because of that, Daisy went to the other location for coverage. "*Good morning, Betty, can you call the crew together? I need to meet with you all before the doors open.*" It was Betty, me, Jackie, Janice, Steve, Luke, Katherine, Roselina, Stephanie, Mora and Nikki. "*Good morning, everyone, I've gathered you all here to first say thank you, thank you all for your service.*" "*Are we losing our jobs?*" Janet said. We all chuckled, and I said, "*No let me finish. Thank you for believing in me, trusting in my vision and being a crucial part of the success we have. Your dedication and faithfulness, I truly appreciate you.*"

"*I'm sure all of you heard about what happened in the lawsuit that has involved myself and the LH VITAMIN. It's a possibility that because of all the men that came forward were patients of mine, there may claim neglect and that I could have put those men at risk. Now there's going to be a nasty trial; you may be called in and asked questions. If so, all I ask is that you tell the truth."* *"I've called Katherine in to ask if she could approve Betty, Stephanie and Doctor Chui to step in during my absence."*

*****

"I know its annual compensation month, so I have approved all increases and it's in Katherine's hands for signature. My LH VITAMIN was outside of P-Body's Clinic; it was only being administered from here. Whatever happens, the clinic and labs would not be affected." Betty instantly got angry. *"This is some bullshit,"* she said. *"Someone is looking for a payday. LH VITAMIN is hot, and folks are looking for any reason to get paid."* They all started to chat, and Steve said that he'd protest all night, whatever it takes. He said, *"Whatever it is they're trying to do, it will not stick. Integrity is all over this place."* *"OK OK, listen, I have not told Daisy the full story surrounding the lawsuit because she will not handle it well, so I'm asking you all to please let me break it to her and during my absence, surround her with love. Please show her that you're there for her and continue making this place great."*

"Doctor Hicks, you sound like you're going somewhere," Jackie said. *"No, I'm just being proactive in all areas. I'll be in and out of court a lot so I'm counting on you all."* I said. *"Yeah, can I talk to you?"* Katherine said. *"OK back to work everyone,"* I grabbed my lab coat and followed Katherine to the back office. *"Talk to me Jay..."* Ohh no, she called me Jay which means she

knows I'm holding back I thought to myself. *"About what Kat?"* I said. *"Don't play with me, please we never kept anything from one another."* I held my head down and started to cry. "I knew it!" she said. *"What happen?"* I started to explain how I got fed up with all the spreading of diseases and then when it hit home…- my girl Elana, I think I just snapped. *"Girl what did you do?"* Katherine pressed. *"OK, I created a serum that initially was supposed to send a burning sensation to the penis with every erection preventing them from wanting sex but I'm guessing I created a monster because the serum deteriorated the penis slowly."* "Girl what!!!?" She yelled. *"Shhhhhh!"* *"What the hell Jay?"*

"What were you thinking?" she pressed. *"I wasn't. I wanted vengeance, I wanted payback, men were destroying women's lives, and they kept coming to me for a temporary fix then continued to spread nasty diseases around,"* I confessed. *"Did you think you wouldn't get caught?"* *"Kat I was careful, the meds combined dissipated after 24 hours, but the constant use of it eventually deteriorated the penis I'm guessing,"* I added. *"Jay, you really did it this time. You work so hard to succeed, you have so much invested… you can lose your license to practice!"*

"I know Kat, I know. I thought about their suit and how I might have to pay each victim I can't move money now; it would be too obvious." She thought for a moment and said, *"I say increase Daisy's salary for yourself, because if it blows up, you'd lose everything and possibly go to jail."* Katherine hugged me, prayed for me and said she'll never leave me. She understood why I did those things; she just didn't think I'd sacrifice our hard work for past hurt to prove a point. My LH Vitamin was successful and now I may have to take it off the shelf. *"Thank you, Katherine, I'm*

sorry I kept this from you. I really didn't want to involve you, because you've work so hard with me to build such a great establishment, I just couldn't involve you."

74

Life is an echo.
What you send out.
Comes back.
What you sow. You reap.
What you give. You get.

~Zig Ziglar~

Chapter **6**

A s we walked out of the office, Jackie fumbled her papers and said, *"Doctor Hicks, Doctor Chui is looking for you."* It felt strange because Doctor Chui asked if she could wait to call me after I was done with our meeting. Her actions were very concerning, and I had hoped she didn't hear anything between Katherine and myself. I saw a couple of patients, wrapped up some paperwork and headed to visit the clinics, where I would see my darling love, Daisy.

"Hey Babe, what are you doing here?" *"Just dropping off supplies to each location and refilling all the vendor machines,*

"Great, I'm almost done, let's finish up together." I thought I could break the news to Daisy, but each time I built up courage, I refused to speak. A picnic came to mind, but Daisy was so tired from the night before we decided to finish our work and head home. Our weekend was amazing; early Saturday morning, I got all our loved ones on the line, did a conference call and asked if we all can meet at Katherine's church. Daisy and I got dressed and I told her to look her best; that I had wanted to take her somewhere special.

Stunning was an understatement. We pulled it up to *Jesus our Lord Baptist Church.* And Daisy looked confused. *"Church Babe?"* she asked. *"You're usually an 'on the couch' kind of gal… watching service at home is your style."* We walked inside and all our friends were staring, then Daisy began to cry. As we walked down the aisles of the church, I whispered to Daisy, *"I love you Baby and this is our time."* Daisy kept crying so I said *stop crying you're going to ruin your makeup."* She was so excited and so was I. Daisy knew what was happening and, on that day, September 3rd, we got married.

*****

Katherine held only one service this day in preparation for what I had planned. Not everyone agreed upon same sex marriage, so I asked if she could marry us after her last service. Katherine and the crew did an amazing job setting up; we couldn't ask for a better day. We all gathered in front of the church and took a group picture, then went to Steak 24, Daisy's favorite place, to celebrate. *Perfect plan* I thought, despite all of what I'm going through, I married the love of my life today and I couldn't be happier.

The next day we had planned to meet with Stephanie. Daisy was so excited for the meet only to show off her ring. "I had to remind her "we're married now" She held up her left ring finger and said, *"You're mine now, so I'm not concerned."* The next day I drove up the hill to Stephanie's office, I was still amazed at the peacefulness it looked. *"Good morning, Stephanie,"* I said. "Good morning, Jaylee, please come in and make yourself comfortable." She shook Daisy's hand and said, "you're as beautiful as Jaylee described. Daisy blushed and said thank you. She had coffee, cake, muffins and hot buttered bread already made as usual. Daisy was in awe from what she seen, her office was beautiful, and Stephanie was well mannered.

Daisy phoned ranged; it was Renee asking her to come into the office right away. Daisy apologized for having to leave and said she will meet me at home. We kissed goodbye and Stephanie and I went into her office.

She had her spread laid out so well, I didn't know if I was in a meeting for my trial or at a spa retreat. She had massage chairs, jazz playing in the background, mimosas with endless food. I figured out later that all of this was for the comfort of her clients. Everyone is always overwhelmed once they get to her office; she wanted them to be relaxed. *"OK let's talk about the elephant in the room,"* she said. *"I'll start with what I know, then you'll tell me what you know about what you're being charged with. Deal?"* she said.

"According to the police report, you are being charged with violently distributing unreasonable standard of care, causing harm to over 40 men by way of contributing to amputation of male

parts. According to the officers, all the men had one thing in common, your LH Vitamins. They made sure to mention that the women involved did in fact have the same disease, but it did not affect their bodies the same as the men."

*****

"The trial scientist took the stand and claimed your vitamins was the cause and is trying to put the pieces together to charge you for it all. Wanting your license revoked, jail time and compensation in the amount of $200,000 per person, plus their attorney fees." I held my head down with sadness, because I knew it was confession time. *"What's wrong Jaylee?"* she asked, *"Is there anything you want to tell me?" "Please be honest; now is the time. This is the only way I can help defend you. Just start from the beginning,"* she said. She sat up in her chair and took out her notepad and pen. *"Stephanie, with all of my accolades, nothing ever compared to the hurt of my past."*

"Rape, molestation, humility, friends who have suffered from the spreading of vicious diseases with a lack of caring, all these things created a monster. My entire life, I wanted to leave a legacy, break generational curses, make my mother proud and provide for my community. Be purposeful in life. Family is important to me, and I knew early on, I would create something so powerful it would help all families in need.

Men are fascinated with our LH Vitamins, hospitals all over requested it, it's passed all the tests and it's been approved by the FDA. Our LH vitamins is my life Stephanie; the one thing I'm the most proud of. I'd never purposely hurt anyone, but I was fed up and wanted revenge. She sat back in her chair with a look of concern. The love of medicine and family is how I got this far, but there was so much wrong in this world I felt I needed to do something about it. I added Cytox to my vitamin," I finally said. *"What's Cytox?"* she asked. *"It is the chemo serum drug that when mixed with the LH vitamin, it supposed to cause a burning sensation with every erection but its caused deterioration to the penis.* "It's almost like someone altered my vitamin, I confessed. Because I didn't see deterioration in the forecast.

*****

"Jaylee, you may have just ruined everything you worked hard for, didn't you know that?" *"Stephanie, I worked on this for years; the added meds dissipate after 24 hours of usage but impact the penis with each use. Honestly, I didn't think I'd ever get caught after being so careful. Each of those men ruined ladies' lives, left them bearing, left them with diseases they couldn't cure. One patient passed it along to their baby. The baby was born with its face burnt on one side from the severity of the disease the mom didn't know she had. The mom said there were no symptoms that was alarming. She thought yeast infections were normal in pregnancies. Stephanie, I was delirious I guess and naïve, to think that I wouldn't be caught."*

"In retrospect, I wish I didn't listen to my selfish thinking, because now I have so much to lose, but mainly the love of my life. I got married yesterday to a beautiful woman who I love and who loves me back. I have not told her yet; I guess I'm just embarrassed and ashamed scared she'd leave. Deceitful huh? Married her without telling her about my past actions. Stephanie leaned in close

to me and said please open to her, be honest don't lose your support system out of embarrassment.

We talked a little more and she assured me then that I'd be fine with what the attorneys were going to submit. They couldn't prove anything, because there was no trace and even with the meds they had found, it could have been from anyone who had visited the lab. She told me that they had no way of proving my involvement, that it would be hard for them to do so. She said I need to just relax, go home and enjoy my new wife. I left there feeling better than when I came; I was so nervous and unsure, but after our talk, and releasing all of that which was bottled up inside, I left feeling better. I grabbed my purse and headed out. I was so excited to share the news, I instantly called Daisy and told her everything.

*****

Days passed without a word either from my attorney or the Sheriff's Office but this morning, as I pulled up to the clinic, something felt different. There were police cars waiting in the lot; officers were talking to Betty, and she was not cooperative. "Good morning, Doctor Hicks, you are under arrest," the officer said. He read me my rights and put me in the police car.

I wasn't as worried, because Stephanie had assured me that even if I was arrested, they had no proof. I didn't resist. I gracefully assured Betty that everything would be OK. Betty shouted irritably, *"I'm calling your attorney, just don't say anything!"* *"She's going to need one,"* said the officer, *because she's under arrest for medical malpractice and manslaughter.* I was processed and asked to turn in all my belongings and was told I'd be able to make a phone call shortly.

I began to panic, *are they processing me? I didn't think they would go this far everyone here looked like criminals. Am I a criminal now?* I thought to myself. They were rough and rigid-looking, but nothing I'd never seen before. As I walked inside the cell, next to me there was a scared woman shivering in the corner. She didn't murmur a word; she only folded her legs up to her chest and continued with her prayer. As they shut the door, I walked towards my bunk and decided to leave her be. Coming to terms with my situation and the possibility of doing time in jail was hard; after about 20 minutes of waiting, they allowed me to make my call.

*****

It's funny, because Daisy's is the only number that I memorized, lucky for me- I thought to myself. *"Daisy, Baby, it's me, I've been arrested. Please don't panic, Stephanie is on the way here. I'll call you when I can, but I need you to stay at the office and supervise the staff. I don't need anyone destroying all that we've worked for, please. I'm OK."* As she cried on the phone, saying how much she loved and missed me, I dropped my head into the base of the phone and said *"Goodbye."* I knew she'd keep the staff lifted during my time away. That's what I loved about her; she'd always found a way to see the good in any bad situation.

"Your attorney is here," Officer Jefferson said. *"Good afternoon, Jaylee,"* Stephanie looked over at me then looked at the officer and said, *"Please leave us."* I then asked, *"What's going*

on, they processed me, charging me with..." but before I could finish, she interrupted me and said, *"...Manslaughter and medical malpractice right." "Please help me understand what's going on, why am I here? I thought there was no proof, there's no way they can detect it."*

"Well, the officer says they have you dead to rights, something about a tape?" she asked curiously. My shocking appearance was obvious, so she said, *"I guess I don't have to ask about a tape, because from the look on your face, it tells me you knew nothing about it." "I have no idea about a tape. Where did the tape come from? What's on the tape? Where did it come from?"* All these questions and no answers. Now I'm frustrated. As Stephanie was about to go into more details, the officer walked in and said to me, "Are you ready to talk now?"

The officer assured me that this was my one chance to come forward, but I assured her I had no idea what she was speaking of. She set the tape recorder on the iron table and pushed play. It was my confession to an unknown person. *Who was my Judas? Who betrayed me?* I thought. This tape was a description of how and what I did in full detail.

*****

As we listened to the tape, Officer Jefferson smiled and asked me, "Is this you?" Before I said anything, Steph jumped in, *"She doesn't have to answer that. This tape needs to be examined by our professional. This could have been altered; there's so much advanced technology these days, your voice could be my voice, could be her voice, how would one know? I was so excited that she intervened, because I was speechless; that was my voice on that tape. It was me explaining all my wrongdoings, but how did they get it? I thought. "If you confess now, we can make a deal, but you must be honest" the officer said.*

"Deal? What kind of a deal?" Stephanie said. We both looked at the officer with great curiosity. She'd be looking at 20 years. My mouth drops, *"Hell no, 20 years for what? You have no proof of her doing anything? Your acquisitions are false. No, no, she won't be accepting that."* Stephanie says. *"OK Jaylee, we're going to ask for 25 years to life and any reasonable additional years for each victim involved,"* the officer said. Our refusal of her deal pissed her off and it showed. Steph turned to me and said, *"Jaylee, I'll try to get you out in the morning. I'll shoot for ROR again, but because you're back here for the same crime, I'm not sure the judge will grant it. "You have got to do something; I can't stay here... you have to Get Me Out of here!"* I said in a panic.

As I headed back to my cell, I replayed that tape in my head; small memories of that day came back to me, but I couldn't remember the 'who', the 'what' or the 'why'. They opened the cell door and there she was again, a young lady sitting in a corner with her knees to her chest, this time she was praying.

Three days had passed, and I hadn't heard anything; right now, I had come to terms with where I was; I wasn't afraid, I just missed everyone. It was phone call time, so I decided to call Attorney Stephanie just to get an update.

*****

"Hello Stephanie Kramer…" "Hey Jaylee, how's it going?" *"So, these last few days, I replayed that tape…Yeah, I know what happened.* We both said at the same time, *'Jackie'. "How'd you know Steph?"* She then replied, *"I played this tape to Katherine who you were talking to at the time, I would not involve her, but she says she remembered both of you seeing Jackie by the door after the meeting was done. Jackie is your Judas,"* she said. *She recorded the conversation, she stated she needed assurance after the speech. What's up with the speech?"* Stephanie asks.

"I thought to bring the team together for an update, because the cops had been asking questions and I knew that would scare the staff. I've always been honest with them, assured them that their job was safe, that there was no need to worry, so I called a meeting and filled them in a bit to calm their anxiety." Oh ok, Stephanie said. Jackie thought she would use it against you if you were to ever fire her, except she got scared of all the police questioning.

Well, "Jaylee, your kindness has gotten you a huge fan base. Folks are already out lobbying on your behalf. I'm going to be honest… from what they are presenting and the tape, it doesn't sound good to me."

The judge denied your bail and scheduled my next court date for two months out. *"My only option now is to prepare a great defense, but I need you to be strong,"* Stephanie said. I was hurt, because I felt I was going to have to get used to where I was for a long time… 25 years… there's no way. *Daisy would have found someone else, thrown me divorce papers, took over my clinics and destroyed my home. I would have lost everything in 25 years. What was I to do?* I jumped on my bunk and cried on the pillow.

It seemed like I had been there forever, but it had only been 30 days. I've managed to keep most of my truths from Daisy until one day she decided to visit me. "Inmate 474244, you have a visitor." I was shocked, because I wasn't expecting anyone and nothing was scheduled for that day. As I walked towards the waiting room, I couldn't help but see that curly haired Latina. *"Babe, what are you doing here?"* I asked. Daisy looked disappointed. *"Are you OK?"* I said. She looked at me and said, *"This is why you never wanted me to visit huh?"*

*****

"You used the fact that you wanted me to stay back and tend to the clinics, but the truth was you didn't want what was on the tape to be exposed to me. I'm your wife," she said. I interrupted her and said, *"That's why I didn't want to tell you, I didn't want you to have to be involved or pressured into anything like going against me." "Cytox Babe?* She said bluntly. I was shocked when she mentioned Cytox, so I said *"Huh?"* She looked at me with anger and said, *"Please don't insult me. During my time in the lab and all those late nights, I eventually put two and two together.* As I went through the story, Daisy began to cry; she was more upset about not knowing than the secret itself. I felt so sorry. She cried and left, and as I called her name, she didn't look back. She just kept walking, *damn... I lost her,* I thought to myself.

Daisy stayed away for a while, and she wouldn't answer my calls. It wasn't until the court date that I saw her. It was her, my mom, Elana, Racquel and Stephanie and a few members of the staff. I was amazed at all the LH VITAMIN supporters that were outside rallying for me. *"Hell, no! Let her go! We need 1.0!"* That's all I heard, lots of chanting. The guy that started this whole ordeal decided that he would drop the charges against his girlfriend, and him and the other forty men decided to start a class action suit against me.

I think they came to terms with it being pointless suing the ladies in the relationship, so they came after me for a big payday. I'd listen to their stories, their testimonials, the back and forth about my creation, about my intention, the things they could find and the things that they couldn't, but then I heard them say Cytox. The very mention of that name made me nervous. The judge asked the attorney to, *"call your first witness."* Mr. Ramon got on the stand then each of the 40 men followed with their stories. When it was time for the cross, Stephanie destroyed each of them with her cross. The case went on so long Judge Allara noticed the time and decided to postpone our session until next Wednesday. I nodded to my family and friends as I headed back to that cold cell.

No Pain is unbearable except that of regret

~Jan Cox Speas~

Judge Allara asked the sheriff to take me back to my cell and once I was inside, I decided to speak to the young lady sitting nervously against the wall. *"Can we please talk? We have been mates for a while and you haven't said a word. Can I ask you a question?"* She looked at me with sadness and said, *"Go ahead."* *"I hear you saying Baruch ata Adonai, Elohein Melech ha-o lam, oseh, ma'asheh breishit. What does that mean?"* I asked. "Blessed are you, Lord our God, King of the universe, maker of the world of creation," She replied. *"Look at where you are?"* I said to her. *"How has that prayer helped your situation?* I asked sarcastically because I couldn't believe that she was so faithful while in jail. *"Do*

you not believe?" she asked. *"I do believe... I watched sermons on TV, but times like these make me question..."* and before I could finish, she said, *"Question what?"*

I couldn't bring myself to say it, so she started to speak and said, *"God is with you always"*. *"I can teach you; I can help you, I could show you how to come to terms with the decisions you've made... I have."* *"Yeah, but look where it led us."* She informed me that I needed to strengthen my relationship with God, that that's the only way to keep hope and to keep going. She and I became close after that conversation. It has always been on in mind to build a relationship with God; I just never had someone to show me different perspectives the way she had. My support system had been amazing; there was always money on my books, calls were accepted and even Daisy answered after I had exhausted all my efforts to reach her. I was sent books, pens and paper just to write. Katherine saw me often, because she was/is my spiritual advisor.

Her visits always left me with lots of hope. She prayed and I ended up feeling better than I had before. After a few days had passed, I started to feel depressed all over again. My cell mate said, *"You have court in two days, and you get to see your attorney tomorrow; let's pray for good vibes and good news.*

*****

Stephanie came to visit me the next day to discuss the plea offer. Jaylee, the attorney wants a 20-year sentence *"If I can get you 10 years, you'll do 6, you'll payout $200,000 to each victim and you would lose your license to practice medicine. Will you accept that?"* I hesitated. With the tape confession, I was at their mercy. *"I'm just not sure I guess." "How did I get here?"* I ask. Arrogance, pride and vengeance led me here. So, I told her I'd think about it but instantly came to my senses and said Yes.

On the day of court, the opposing attorney called Dr. Simpson to the stand and his testimony won over the jury. He stated facts, brought visuals and statistics. He brought up how Cytox can affect the body and that he had found it in my lab. As brilliant as he was, they were unable to prove that it was the main cause, as it was not found in their system and the medicine could've come from anywhere or anyone. They even tested each victim and nothing was found.

Dr. Simpson tried convincing every one of his findings, but nothing would stick, so their attorney pulled a rabbit out of the hat. He pulled out the confession tape to play for the jury and they were shocked. It was Steph's turn to speak; her rebuttal of how illegal it was to record a private conversation on top of the men having nothing in their system, put the jury on the fence. My case went on for hours and both sides knew the jury was 50/50, so they came up with a plea that would satisfy both sides.

They offered me. 10 years (serving 6 years) $200,000 paid out to each victim, pay their attorney fees and I would lose my license to practice medicine. *"Everyone please stand,"* the bailiff said. As Judge Allara entered the courtroom and sat behind the desk, she instructed us all to be seated. Judge Allara looked at the small, folded paper on her desk then she said, *"It has come to my attention that there is a plea."*

*****

"Yes, your honor," says Attorney Jones. *"Doctor Hicks has agreed to a guilty plea. 10 years, serving 6, to payout $200,000 to each victim, and to turn over her medical license, where she will be no longer able to practice medicine."* The crowd made a disappointing sigh, then Judge Allara banged her gavel and asked everyone to please be quiet in her courtroom. Daisy lowered her head while Racquel and Elana comforted her. I had promised to never hurt Daisy, but from the look in her eyes, she was hurt a great deal.

"Are you pleading guilty to this offense Judge Allara asked. *"Yes I am." "Do you understand what you're pleading to?" "Yes, I do,"* I said reluctantly. *"Was this agreement made under duress?" "No ma'am, it wasn't." "OK, then I sentence you to 10 years in jail at the Bridgetown County prison for women, where you'll serve a maximum of 10 years and a minimum of six years. You'll pay each victim listed in this case $200,000 in punitive damages and you'll turn over your medical license, and you're no longer able to practice medicine. This court is adjourned."*

Daisy ran to hug me before the bailiff took me away and she whispered, *"I will be seeing you soon."* She smelled so good, all I could think about was her love for champagne toast bodywash. *Would she wait for me?* I thought. *It might be selfish to even wish for it.* So many questions ran through my mind as I walked away from her that day. I said my goodbyes to my mom and friends and wished everyone well. Six years is a long time, but it could have been more.

Fast forward into my sentence, I made prison friends and kept myself busy. I'd watch the ladies play cards for fun. They talk about all the different situations they encountered, but the one lady I was interested in was the one everyone feared. She was so angry yet looked so sad. I know it's crazy of me, but I had to talk to her; I wasn't afraid. The ladies would warn me, *"Don't go over there leave her alone!"* But Daredevil Jaylee just had to go over. Interesting enough, she turned out to be really kind, just misunderstood. She was suffering from depression because before going inside, she was in the process of gender transition... At least that's what the ladies tell me. So, I walked over and introduced myself; she held her head up and gave me the dirtiest look.

"If you ever need someone to talk to or need any medical advice, feel free to come to my cell. I just wanted to introduce myself; I didn't come to cause problems. I'll leave you to it." So, I walked off and went back to playing cards. The next day, she came to my cell; I'm guessing it was to intimidate me. After she heard about my medical experience and 2.0 she changed how she spoke to me, and we became friends. I helped him (her pronoun) financially to keep up with his hormones and because my specialty was the male body, I helped in ways that he had never heard of.

I became known all over the prison. Even though I couldn't practice medicine outside prison walls it didn't stop me from helping those that I could inside. I would advise and explain areas that were tough for them to understand. I spent most of my days in the library; I took many jobs in the prison to stay busy, the medical office specifically. Jail was challenging, but I adjusted. My cellmate never changed her routine; she prayed and prayed, and we talked more and more. I respected her faith and began to research my own. As a kid, I just went to church, never really paid much attention, really didn't understand the message, and I was always sleepy and very hungry.

I used to think God gave up on me, because even as a young girl or shall I say a small child, I'd experience so much bad. God allowed every man in my life to show their perversion; to look at me as something they could just use and toss away. My innocence was taken at such a young age, so much manipulation, how I view relationships, how I thought it was always my fault. They were so mean afterwards. I used to think, *how can you take something so precious from a young girl or from anybody for that matter and then treat them horribly when it's over?*

I don't know; I tried to lock all those feelings up and attach reason to them, but there's never a good reason to molest anyone. Could it be that my father started my madness, of course it was? He never showed me what it meant in terms of love and being loved. I guess I just looked for love in all the wrong places, some by choice, some by force.

*****

Authority figures, educated men, police officers, firefighters-those are the type of men I would seek out, ignoring all their red flags… oh and did I mention I liked them much older than myself? Talk about daddy issues. Folks will say 'daddy issues' and I'd say that's an understatement. *My dad is a horrible man,* I thought. *Was my mom not enough? Why did he hurt me that way? Could he have been that desperate?* According to the rumors, my dad had so much street respect. Everyone feared him, everyone adored him and with all the respect he was given no one ever expected his daughter laid hurt by his hands.

I used to want answers to those questions, and it wasn't until I went to college, I just gave up. I learned to distract myself by planting all my time in my schoolbooks; not too bad though; I became a successful doctor through all my troubles.

My cell mate was so faithful to her routine throughout her time in jail and at times I'd get jealous. I decided I would go to the TV room and watch my girl Katherine preach. Her services were every Sunday at 3 PM. What I loved the most was that she was on YouTube, and I was able to subscribe to her channel. I could watch her any time I wanted just by pressing the reply. Katherine mastered the learning of theology, the way she would break down the word made me see things so different. I learned how to really listen to the message then apply it to my own life. I guess that's the difference between listening to it as a child than as an adult. It becomes more than just words you hear; they become a message you have to listen to catch it. Once you catch it, you must apply it.

Now I know there's folks that look at homosexuality as a sin. Katherine never shunned me out or judged me. She never flat out said she accepted it, but she never said I wasn't worthy of God's love. My relationship with God is not to be judged by anyone. Kat would always make sure I knew that, and she always made sure to tell me how much she loved me. At this point I had been locked up for 2 years without visits. One day, I heard the guards say *"Inmate 474422, you have a visitor."*

*****

Elana and Racquel were in the waiting room. Seeing me shackled like a dog, my girls began to cry. They sat me to the table, made sure my hands didn't move and made it clear to say, *"no touching"*. *"Y'all bitches crying?"* I said. While Elana was sniffling, she couldn't get it out, but eventually said, *"Bitch you shouldn't be in here, you should be out healing folks."* *"No ladies, I'm right where I'm belong. I did some horrible things and for that, I've lost everything. This six-year sentence is the time and what I need to get the therapy that will help me be ok with it all. To help forgive myself for all the harm I've caused. I can justify my actions, but I won't because I was wrong, "* I said.

"Elana, I want to apologize, Mr. Ramon as I know him and Ralpfy to you for not doing more. It was me that caused his injuries. I had no idea you two were dating until it was the end. Please forgive me for not doing more. The hurt these men have caused and then getting away with it all... I guess I was just tired of watching women get hurt by the hands of spineless men." *"Jay, I love you and we know anything you've done was to protect women. OK enough with the mushy shit, Racquel said. How are you? Are you sleeping with the jail hottie?"* Racquel said.

"No, girl, I'm mentoring and building my faith." *"That's awesome, "* Elana said. *"I heard Katherine and Daisy fired Jackie's ass, "* she said. *"Yeah, she was my Judas, "* I said disappointingly. *"She set me up and that's the real reason I'm here, well partly the reason. I don't know, I guess when you do wrong, wrong has to come back; this is my payback.* We chatted another 10 minutes then we heard *Inmate 474422- time's up.* *"OK ladies, hold it down out there for me, keep an eye on my Daisy and pray that my hard work with LH VITAMIN is not forgotten."*

"That will never die girl; everyone is protesting to keep your vitamin on the shelves, Daisy is working hard making sure no one forgets your creation." "I love you, see you at the next visit," I said, as the guards shackled me up and led me back to my cell. I watched my friends weep for me and all I wanted to do was hug them, *four more years and I'm out.* That's all I can say to myself to keep going. *I'll still be fine in four years, especially doing 100 squats a day, my booty is going to be plump I thought.*

*****

"Inmate 474422, another visit." I'm loving today already I *said to myself.* As I walked back to the waiting area, there was Stephanie and Katherine sitting at the table in the lobby waiting for me to come down. We chatted a bit and then I had to ask, *"Steph, are you here on a professional level or you are just happy to see me?"* *"No Jaylee, Katherine and I are here to give you an update and extend your visitations."* *"Give me an update? What's the tea?"* I asked. *"Daisy had been MIA for a while, but we later found out that she's been in the lab and promoting your vitamins all over town., She even created you a social media platform where it went viral."* Viral? I asked. *"Yes viral, both men and women have been commenting on the decisions to keep the vitamin on the shelf, so things are looking good*

"Everyone loves you Jay," Katherine said. *"Your fans started a GOFUNDME account so you can continue your research when you come home. There are investors that are willing to jump on board to get you back out there."* I started to tear up, because I didn't realize just how many people I've inspired. *"We know the judge ordered the vitamins to be removed everywhere, but if you*

sell the product and give up the rights, then the vitamins could live on." "Wait what?" I said. "That's my baby though." "Yes," Steph said, "but you can't do anything with it; even your clinics and any affiliates cannot use it unless it's being produced by another company."

"Listen to the offer before you reject it," Katherine said. "Give up ownership of my baby?" I asked. "Yes, give up ownership and they'll pay you out $10 million up front, $500,000 a year to keep the name and they'll fund any research you decide to do or come up with when you return home." "That's the deal," Katherine said. *"You've lost all your clinics except the lab. Due to the mini payouts from this, the attorney fees and all... we had to liquidate to help you, and Daisy stay afloat. We put half of your funds into overseas investments. You'll be OK financially;" "So this is the reason both you came up here?" "Yes and no; we both miss you and we both want the best for you. I'm your friend Jay. I'll never betray you; sign the papers and I'll get things in motion."*

"Let me think about it and get back to you tomorrow?" "For sure, I'll be back here first thing in the morning with all your paperwork." I trusted Katherine, and as much as I didn't want to believe it, they both were right. The settlement was a great deal - 10 mil up front and 500K a year for the next 10 years, not a bad idea. Maybe I'll do more research once I'm home; after all, I still have the lab. *"Damn,"* was all I could say.

As I walked in my cell, I heard God say to me, *'vengeance is mine and you tried it for yourself.'* Then I heard God say, *'greed will leave you empty'* Just as they were about to slam the bars behind me a sound came from the corner; it was my cell mate, asking if I wanted to pray. I politely declined and told her I already had prayer time, and I needed to get to know God myself. Establish a true relationship with God but *thank you for always guiding me and showing me the light,"* I said. *"I'll always be here,"* she said. I cried in my pillow that night, because God spoke to me and I finally listened.

The next day, Steph came back as she promised. I signed the settlement papers as agreed. My current business had the funds to handle the payment to cover the victims. I also gave everybody a severance pay, a nice one too, to start over so that when I'm home I will be debt free. The guard opened my cell gate, and as I walked inside, I asked the guard, *"Where's my cell mate?* The guard responded, *"Jay, you never had a cellmate. They had you isolated from the general population due to your crime."* "No, no," I said, *"She would always stay in a corner praying over there, right over there I pointed."* *"No Jay, there were days we'd walk pass listening to talk to yourself, but we thought, maybe that's just something you did to cope with your sentence.*

"Are you sure, I've been all alone in this cell for the past 2 years?" *"We're sure, you've been here all alone."* As they took my shackles off, I walked to my bed, lay facing my pillow and I cried again. Not only did God speak to me, but GOD was with me and has been with me this entire time.

*****

"Inmate 474422, you have a visitor." Who could this be? Did I forget to sign something? Could they be back with more news? As I got closer to the waiting area, I saw my Daisy. The guards took off the shackles and sat me at the table, giving strict instructions not to move my hands. She looked so beautiful—her body was to die for—and the way my name rolled off her tongue just drove me wild. I had told the guards she was my wife, so because we were *married*, we were allowed to kiss. Man, oh man, did I miss her kiss. We chatted, and she seemed so happy. Daisy always made sure to remind me that she was my number one fan— and I believed her. She was handling so much out in the world, I thought. *I can't wait to get home and give her the world.* Twenty minutes passed, and I knew our time was almost up. I heard the guard yell, "Hicks, your time is up!" Daisy leaned in and whispered, "Baby, I got you." I didn't know what she meant by that. Then she said it again, "Baby, I got you, LH 3.0." "3.0?" I thought. *What is that?* I asked. She gave me a evil smirk, stood up from her chair, and walked away. I pointed at her and yelled, "guard! "My Daisy was behind it all…….

Message from the Author

Psalm 147:3

"He healeth the broken in heart and bindeth up their wounds".

Acknowledgments

First, I'd like to give praise and honor to my Heavenly Father.

Without His daily presence, His constant reminders of how blessed I am,

And the creativity He has placed within me, none of this would be possible.

I would also like to acknowledge my husband, my children, and my mom, who have All been incredibly supportive of my dreams. I must say—they are my rock.